A Winter's Promise

Book One in
**The Never Miss a Sunset
Pioneer Family Series**

Previously published as
All the Days After Sunday

Jeanette Gilge

LIFEJOURNEY
BOOKS

David C. Cook Publishing Co.
Elgin, Illinois • Weston, Ontario

LifeJourney Books is an imprint of David C. Cook Publishing Co.

David C. Cook Publishing Co., Elgin, Illinois 60120
David C. Cook Publishing Co., Weston, Ontario

A WINTER'S PROMISE (formerly *All the Days After Sunday*)
© 1988 by Gilge, Jeanette

Edited by LoraBeth Norton
Illustration by Ben Wohlberg
Cover Design by Dawn Lauck

First printing, 1988
Printed in the United States of America
92 91 90 89 88 87 5 4 3 2 1

Gilge, Jeanette.
 A winter's promise/Jeanette Gilge.
 p. cm.
 ISBN 1-555-13465-3
 I. Title.
PS3557.I3525W56 1988   88-2239
813'.54—dc19   CIP

Contents

One

The Homestead in Winter

The wind howled around the corner of the cabin, sending a shiver down Emma's back and out to her very fingertips. She stretched to light the kerosene lamp high on the bracket against the log wall.

"Must be ten below," she muttered as she pulled on her heavy woolen coat and beckoned to little Albert. He shuffled toward her, intent on fastening two clothespins together.

"You watch baby George," she whispered, "and don't let Fred climb on *anything*, and keep Ellie out of the water pail." She bent closer. "Take good care of them and Saturday, when Papa comes home, I'll tell him what a big boy you are."

"Is Saturday after I sleep?"

"No. This is Thursday. Two more sleeps and it's Saturday."

Albert grinned. "And Papa comes home!"

She hugged him. "That's right! Now you watch the little ones real good, and I'll be back in a little while."

Casting a furtive glance at three-year-old Fred and Ellie, seventeen months, who were wrestling like two puppies under the table, Emma tied her *kopf tuch* snug, picked up the lantern, and slipped out the door. Baby George, three months old, had just finished nursing. He'd sleep—unless Ellie rocked the cradle too hard.

Emma didn't mind doing chores while Al was away working all week in the lumber camp. The barn with its warm-animal smells was a welcome change from the dark cabin, though it, too, was dark. But it was leaving the three little ones in five-year-old Albert's care three times a day that knotted her stomach.

The taunting wind tore at her coat as Emma slogged toward the barn. It wrenched the door out of her hands as soon as she unlatched it. She tugged the door shut behind her, her heart thumping, and groped for the lantern in the dusk. She lit it and hung it on a nail covered with sparkling frost crystals. Another time she would have taken a moment to admire the diamond crusting adorning every nail, bolt, and hinge, but not tonight. She hurried to give the noisy chickens their steaming hot water; it would be cold in seconds and frozen before they could finish drinking it. *Poor things, with their frostbitten combs*, Emma thought. *They're as tired of winter as I am, and it's only the first week of February.* She grunted as she dragged a pitchfork full of hay toward the ox.

For a moment Emma wished they were living in town again, so Al could be home every night, and she wouldn't have to leave the little ones alone like this. But only for a moment. She hadn't forgotten what living in town had done to Al.

In the early days of their marriage, on their little northern Wisconsin homestead, Al had always been full of bright-eyed banter, no matter how hard he worked. After they moved to Phillips—temporarily, in hopes of saving enough money for taxes and a team of horses for the farm—it was as though the day's work spared him barely enough energy to drag himself home, dull-eyed and sullen. And month after month, the cost of necessities ate up all but a few crumbs of his wages.

Now, as she dragged hay to the cows, Emma remembered the February day a year ago when Al had sat scribbling on a sheet of figures.

He had thrown his stub of a pencil across the table and asked, "Emma? What say we move back home?"

She didn't remember what she had answered, she'd been so taken by surprise, but they had talked way past their usual bedtime and decided that, if they were going to move back, they should do it in the spring. All that next day, pictures had flashed through her mind's eye. She could see the little ones running across the slope of the field toward the cedar swamp, the curve of the river below the house, blue-green cabbage leaves with raindrops dancing on them, dew-covered grass sparkling in the morning sun.

That day she had admitted to herself how much she despised the clatter of heavy boots on the board sidewalk close to the front window, the dust that rolled up from the alley and settled on her nice clean wash each time a buggy went by, the constant scolding of the gravel-voiced woman to the east and the whining of the one to the west. And worst of all, the constant fear that one of the little ones would get out of the fenced-in yard and into the busy street.

The more she thought about the homestead, the more she wanted to go back. Were the forget-me-nots still there under the south window and the Wind Lake roses still alive? In town there was little she could do to help Al, except care for the house and children and tend a tiny garden in summer. On the farm she could do much more.

She would miss going to church, of course. She'd miss being with people who loved the Lord, and she'd certainly miss the singing, but most of all she'd miss having the pastor's words to think about during the week. But Al said he planned to get the neighbors together and see about finding a pastor to come—maybe only once a month at first. She'd keep praying, and one day they'd have their own church.

Oh, and it would be good to be near her father and mother and Winnie and Walter and Dick—and the Gebers. Mrs. Geber had helped deliver Albert and Fred, but Ellie had been born in town. The doctor who had delivered her had been in a hurry, because he had another woman in labor on the other end of town. He'd been impatient, to say the least. It would be good to have Mrs. Geber's help with the next one.

Emma had been ready to start packing immediately—until she happened to glance across the street and see the Riley children cavorting in the snow. "What will I do without Mrs. Riley?" she had said right out loud.

When Fred fell downstairs and cut his chin, when Al got a sliver under his thumbnail, when Ellie cried so hard she turned blue, and goodness knows how many other times, Emma had called for Kate Riley. Each time, Kate's light-hearted wisdom had set Emma's world straight again. And it wasn't just in times of crisis. Emma couldn't count the times the two women had run across that street to share some comical or touching incident as well.

Remembering, Emma leaned on the pitchfork a moment. What she would give to hear Kate Riley's laugh right now, and to see that warm glow of approval in her eyes. She could picture Kate as she looked when Emma told her they were moving back to the homestead, the light from the kitchen window catching the coils of her red hair.

"Sure 'n' I'll be missin' you, girl. But 'tis back with the trees 'n' the river you should be," she had said, all the while tucking stray locks of Emma's hair into her pug as though Emma were one of her daughters. Emma had wanted to bury her head in Kate's shoulder and sob but, seeing three pairs of little eyes needing assurance, she had mustered a smile instead and filled the teapot.

"What's the matter with me!" Emma scolded herself. "Here I stand daydreaming while the little ones are alone!" She hurried back for another load of hay. But again, as she dragged more hay to the cows, her mind slipped back. It was just such times as these winter days that Al had warned her about that night over the blue-checked oilcloth. They simply had to have *some* money, so he would have to work in the lumber camp in winter. It would mean he'd be gone all week, every week, and she would have to do the milking and take care of the livestock.

Emma had felt so brave then, when she assured Al she could do it. Why hadn't she thought about the loneliness or the cold or the hazards of leaving four little children in the house on their own?

They moved back in May. That first day back on the farm had been one of the happiest days of their lives. In spite of being weary from the all-day trip, Emma had explored all around the house and barn, carrying little Ellie while the boys trailed behind her like ducklings. While Al and Grandpa Verleger unloaded the wagon, she had found the forget-me-nots under tall weeds and the Wind Lake roses with their tiny green sprouts. She could hardly wait till morning to tear out the dry weeds that choked them.

That night, lying on their straw mattress listening to the river—their river—she and Al had agreed that it was the pleasantest sound in the world. Emma never wanted to leave their homestead again, no matter how hard things became.

She had planted a big flower garden while Al planted potatoes, oats, corn and rutabagas. Then he had worked at home, cutting wood and clearing land, until after Christmas, so Emma could regain her strength after George was born in late November.

Emma served Molly a fork full of hay. "Eat good, mama cow. Grow a big, strong calf," she urged as she went on remembering.

She thought of the first time she had seen their house. The walls were up, but the roof wasn't on. Emma had stood by the south window opening and squealed, "Oh! I can see right down on the river!"

Al had come up behind her and gathered her in his arms. "You like that?"

"You know I do."

"Remember once when we were walking along the creek at your folks' place, you said you loved the sound of running water and you'd like to have a house by a river where you could hear the water—and see it, too?"

She turned and nuzzled her face into his neck. "And you remembered!"

Emma dragged more hay, recalling the many ways Al had found to delight her. It was almost a womanlike quality, but it made him more of a man, not less, in her eyes. Maybe, she mused, he could risk being thoughtful and tender because he had no doubts about his own manhood. He was respected by the other men not only for his physical strength and intelligence, but for his honesty and loyalty as well. And he'd certainly had no trouble attracting girls—especially Millie Luft, that hussy!

Silly goose! Why ever are you thinking about that now!

Emma finished feeding the cows and rested her head against patient Molly's flank while she stripped her. A few more days and Molly, waiting for her calf, would be dry like Bessie. Good thing Cora was still milking, cross old thing though she was. No wonder Grandpa Verleger had insisted they have her. Even this morning, when he had come by to see how Emma and the children were, he had insisted that Cora was a good cow. Emma knew better than to disagree with him. Besides, she was grateful for the milk.

Before she started to milk Cora, she scratched a peep-hole in the window frost so she could see the house. Every time she came to the barn she had the same argument with herself. Should she run back halfway through her chores and see how the children were doing, or quickly finish her work so she could go back and stay in with them?

Emma sighed and hurried over to Cora with stool and pail. Before she had even set the stool in place, Cora's hind leg shot out and kicked her on the thigh. Emma reeled backwards, and the pail and stool—and Emma—clattered to the floor. She gasped as the pain raced up her spine.

"*Dumm esel!*" she wailed. "Just because I'm in a hurry!" She tried to get up, but her legs wouldn't move. She rolled toward a post and pulled herself up on her knees. Her head was spinning, and she shook so violently it was hard to hold onto the post. She grunted and strained, but her legs refused to move. "Father! Help me!" she sobbed. The thought came, *This is like when you hit your elbow or knee—your "crazy" bone. Just wait.*

She sagged down a moment into a pain-filled world, thinking about the little ones waiting for her in the house.

"Try again!" she ordered her body.

Slowly . . . shakily . . . she stood.

"O Lord, thank you!" she whispered. "Help me milk the cow. Please help me."

Breathing hard, Emma righted the stool, retrieved the pail, and edged cautiously around Cora. "You old cow, you!" she sobbed. "I didn't even touch you!" She sat down with a groan and tried to hold the pail between her knees. It slipped to the floor.

"I've got to do it!" she told herself. "Albert can't milk, and he's too little to go for help in this cold."

Clenching her jaws to keep her teeth from chattering, she prayed, "Please, God, send Grandpa Verleger or one of the Gebers—somebody!"

She wedged the pail between her knees again and squeezed hard. The pressure made her gasp with pain, but she managed to hold on At first her hands refused to obey her, but she took a deep breath, tried again, and heard the streams of milk hit the bottom of the pail.

There seemed to be no end to Cora's milk tonight. As the pail grew heavier, Emma's pain increased until her tears ran again. But Emma gritted her teeth and kept milking. When Cora was finally dry, Emma sidled away, keeping a wary eye on those hind legs.

Usually she carried the lantern in one hand and the pail of milk in the other. Tonight, she decided, it would be all she could do to carry the milk. She blew out the lantern, left it in the barn, and set the pail out the door ahead of her.

The wind fought for the door again, but Emma got behind it, leaned all her weight against it, and slammed the bar in place. As she did so she realized that she had left her mittens in the barn. But the lights of the cabin beckoned, and she chose to endure cold hands rather than fight the wind again. She staggered a few steps, lost her balance, and fell. She couldn't see how much milk she had spilled, but the pail still felt quite heavy.

Emma got to her feet, took a few more painful steps, and fell again when her legs went weak under her. "Why didn't I go back for mittens?" she wailed as she tried to pull her hands up into her sleeves to protect them.

Once more she struggled to her feet. By now the milk was nearly gone. There would be more in the morning—if she could get back to the barn—but the little ones needed milk tonight. She couldn't risk spilling more. There was only one way. Emma set the pail ahead of her and inched her way toward it.

Her coat kept getting in the way and, when it pulled open, ice cut her knees. With every movement, pain shot up her back and down her legs, but she kept crawling. Over and over she set the pail ahead of her, and laboriously made her way to it. She thought of the countless times she had hurried back and forth on this path on strong legs, never thinking about the distance from house to barn.

She looked up at the dim light, still so distant, then turned her head away from the wind and crawled like a mechanical, grunting thing. She couldn't feel the pail handle anymore, but somehow she managed to keep setting it ahead, setting it ahead.

Again she gauged the distance to the light. It didn't seem that she had moved at all. *I'll just rest a moment*, she told herself, and laid her head on her arm. *Just like a great big warm featherbed*, she thought. She would rest a while and then crawl some more.

The children! What's the matter with me? she scolded herself. *I've got to keep on going. No resting now!*

Summoning every last bit of energy, she set the pail ahead of her and crawled. Again. Again. "Lord, help me!" she called into the howling wind. She didn't dare look to see how far she had to go. *Move!* she ordered her body. *Move!* She knew she'd stay on the path; snowbanks bordered it on either side.

The light was close now. Dark wall dead ahead. Set the pail down. Once more. Once more.

Emma pulled herself to her feet at the door of the lean-to with a sob of relief and stumbled in the door, blinking, panting, looking for the children.

She heard them before she saw them. As soon as they felt the rush of cold air, they dashed toward her. Thankful that their squeals drowned out her groans, she reeled against the wall. When she got her balance, she plunged her hands into cool water.

"If I can just get the little ones to bed," she whispered.

"I know there are other things to do, but I can't think—"

The stove! Got to keep the fire burning.

She wrapped her stiff hands in the roller towel a moment and then clumsily picked up a stick of wood. "Albert!" she called. "Lift the stove lid for me."

He lifted it cautiously, but still she warned, "Careful now! Don't drop the poker." When she had loaded in several sticks of wood, she said, "Good boy! Put it back on."

Albert frowned up at her. "Mama? You hurt?"

She nodded. "I fell. Hurt my back. You'll have to help me get the little ones to bed."

His lip trembled.

"There! There! Don't cry! I'll be fine in the morning," she whispered. "You help me now!"

She sat down to take off her overshoes and cried out in agony.

Only Albert heard her.

"Got to be careful how I sit down," she explained, managing a smile. "Go get cups . . . and bread . . . and the syrup."

Off he went, glancing back apprehensively over his shoulder.

She felt her stockings sticking to her knees and saw that spots of blood had soaked through her dress. She was thankful that the light was too dim for the children to notice.

With trembling hands Emma poured the milk into cups as the children clamored around her. There was half a cup for each and a little for herself. She took a swallow, but her stomach threatened to revolt. Maybe later she could drink it.

While the children munched their bread and syrup, she put more wood in the stove. She could grasp the poker now, but the pain in her hands as the circulation returned overshadowed the pain in her thigh and tail bone.

A tear splashed on the hot stove and sizzled. *Please, Lord, help me stop crying. Please take this awful pain away. I've got to keep going and get the children to bed.*

Teeth clenched, guarding against a sudden groan, Emma washed little hands and faces, answered questions, tugged at tight sleeves, and fumbled with buttons. When they were all in their flour-sack nightgowns, she kissed them, tolerated their hugs, and shooed them off to bed.

But Fred whined, the baby began to cry, and Ellie clung to her, pleading to be rocked.

Emma hugged her. "Albert will sing to you, *Liebchen.* Mama has to feed baby Georgie."

Albert dragged Ellie off to bed, and reluctantly she cuddled in between the boys. *"Du, du liegst mir im Hertzen,"* Albert sang, and Ellie twirled a yarn knot in the comforter with her chubby little finger.

"Shh . . . Mama'll feed you right now," Emma crooned to the baby as she changed him. Only four diapers left. She had planned to wash diapers tomorrow, but how could she possibly carry the water?

With George in her left arm, she unbuttoned her dress and sat down in the rocker. Albert heard her gasp.

"Mama?"

"It's all right!" she giggled. "I just forgot I'd hurt my sitter."

He giggled, too.

She winked at him from the doorway on her way to the bed, and he began to sing again.

Even lying still, the pain throbbed. She hoped the baby wasn't aware of the tension in her body.

How can I get the diapers washed? Maybe tomorrow someone will come. Father, she prayed, *please send someone to help me.*

She knew one way to make diaper washing easier— she would line those last four diapers with clean soft rags that she could burn in the stove. It was a temporary measure—she'd soon run out of rags, too—but for now it would have to do.

Her thoughts rushed to the other tasks ahead of her. The cattle had to be fed and watered. Now that the river ice was too thick for them to reach the water, she had to hoist buckets of water up for them. She groaned at the thought. And she'd have to milk Cora, too.

Surely someone will come, she encouraged herself. *Someone will come.*

Two

Night of Pain

Eight leaden bongs floated through the rooms from the pendulum clock. Emma heard none of them. Nine. Then ten. Still she slept.

The baby stirred, and Emma's eyes flew open. The house was quiet. Too quiet! All she could hear was the tick, tick of the clock and the howl of the relentless wind.

"Oh, my goodness! The stove!" she whispered, as she rolled over and tucked the baby in his cradle beside her bed. She tried to get up, but a stab of pain sent her groaning back onto the pillow.

Jaws clenched, she forced herself up and clutched chair backs for support as she made her way to the stove. Not a crackle. Teeth chattering, Emma crumpled paper and tucked in slim sticks of kindling wood. "How could you go out?" She berated the cold black stove, feeling as though a trusted friend had abandoned her.

She struck a wooden match and watched the precious paper disappear. *Only a little left. Hope Al brings a newspaper when he comes home.*

Ignoring her pain, Emma hovered over the fragile flames, feeding new wood into the stove as the fire gained strength until it reared healthily up the chimney. The frost, she noticed, had crept up to the very top of the windows.

In the children's room she pulled the covers high around their heads. Many times she had wished Ellie could have a room of her own, but tonight she was glad that all three were cuddled together in one bed.

Again she fed the fire, aware that she could put off tending her knees no longer. She brought her medicine box from the pantry and poured warm water from the teakettle into the washbasin. Perched on the edge of a chair, Emma mercilessly peeled the stockings from her knees and let them sag around her ankles, wincing in pain as she bathed the bleeding spots.

Her nose wrinkled as she tried to apply some of Grandpa Verleger's vile-smelling brown salve. Although Grandpa had never had any medical schooling, his own studying had given him the status of neighborhood medical "expert." The ointment slid off the seeping wounds, so Emma spread it on scraps of rags, laid them on her knees, and wrapped bandages around them. She would need to roll more the next time she ironed. (Grandpa had taught her to how to prepare bandages from muslin, too.)

Expertly she wound the bandage around her leg, snug, but not so tight as to hinder movement. She tore the last few inches of the strip in half lengthwise, then wound one part in one direction, one the other, and tied them where they met.

After she had undressed and pulled on her nightgown, she wedged another stick of wood into the stove, adjusted the draft, and blew out the lamp. Then, disgustedly, she lit it again it. She had forgotten to wind the clock.

Finally in bed, jaws clenched against the pain, Emma thought how thankful she was to be there. The stove was full, the clock wound. . . . The geranium! It would freeze if she left it on the windowsill.

"Oh, why didn't I think of that when I wound the clock?" she chided herself. For days she had watched a fat bud-cluster emerge, and today she had seen brilliant red peeping through a crack.

"I just can't get up again," she muttered into her pillow.

But the remembrance of that red cluster of blossoms that had bloomed at Christmas came back to her. It had glowed comfortingly even in the lamp light, and in the sunlight it had fairly danced. How many times a day had her eyes sought it out—the only spot of color amid the wood-browns and grays.

For a little while the bed's solace and the flower's beauty hung in the balance.

Beauty won.

Keeping the red blossom in her mind's eye, Emma groaned her way to the window, set the flower pot on the table, and hobbled back to bed. She couldn't stop shivering, and her stomach felt sick. She rolled Al's pillow tight against it.

Oh, Al! If only you'd come home! Maybe he'd sense something was wrong. *Foolish thought! I've got to face it! I'll have to get up and do chores before the little ones wake up.*

The baby usually woke about five. Emma would nurse him, he'd go back to sleep, and she could slip out to do the chores before the others woke. But now she could rest, except to get up every hour or so to put wood in the stove. It was odd how her built-in alarm clock alerted her hourly all winter but allowed her to sleep in summer— except tonight, when she had been unusually exhausted.

Emma wriggled into a more comfortable position, expecting the sting of her freshly dressed wounds to ease any moment. But that position hurt her bruised thigh, so she moved again. The next position hurt her back.

"I'll think of something pleasant," she told herself, "and I'll go right to sleep."

Spring! First there'd be mayflowers in the woods, then trilliums, then violets all along the riverbanks. Al would spade a plot for her garden, and she'd watch for the tiny green sprouts and teach the little ones the name of each plant. She could see the deep red soil and the rows of green after she had finished hoeing them. And Al would clear more land. On, how he would work! One night he'd light the pile of brush and logs, and they'd feel the heat of it all the way to the cabin.

The waste bothered her, and she had told Al so last spring. "I know we need fields for crops, but it takes so long for a tree to grow. It's a shame to see all that good wood burn—enough to heat every home in Phillips all winter."

Al had chuckled. "What you want me to do? Can't sell it. Can't burn it all for firewood."

She knew he was right, but that awful waste still bothered her.

Emma turned over carefully and sighed. *I suppose I'll feel the same way when I see that fire this spring. If only there was some way to use all that good wood.*

But spring wouldn't come for a long while. A chill raced through her, and a knot of fear lodged in her stomach. It would be only a matter of time before this pain would be gone and she would be able to work comfortably again. But what if she had *another* accident? What if the little ones had an accident while they were alone in the house?

I'll have to take them to the barn with me, she reasoned. *I'll bundle baby George up —take the oval clothes basket out to the barn and put him in that. He'll probably cry the whole while, but at least he'll be safe. And Ellie?* Emma sighed. *She'll be into everything. Can I count on Albert to watch her and Fred while I work? He's only five. He gets interested in what he's doing. I'll have to carry the baby and Ellie out there and back. Al-bert can carry the water for the chickens, but I'll have to make another trip back for the milk. Oh, dear! I'll be all worn out running back and forth. What if it storms? Or gets down to twenty or thirty below zero?*

She allowed the same thoughts to circle through her mind again.

No! Taking them along to the barn won't work. I'm going to tell Al he'll just have to stay home. We'll manage, somehow, without the money from the lum-ber camp.

But if there was no money, she knew, there would be no horses. No horses, no trips to see Pa and Ma. Tears threatened again. No money, no sewing machine. Each year it was harder to sew all those clothes for the chil-dren by hand. And the taxes—they had to have money for taxes. And shoes for all of them. She could knit and sew, but she couldn't make shoes.

The clock struck twelve. A precious hour gone, and she hadn't even begun to rest.

"Got to stop worrying. Got to stop worrying," Emma muttered to the pillow. "I'll think of some songs.... 'When the roll is called up yon-der,' " she hummed, but the words didn't make her feel better at all. She had a lot of living to do before she was ready for that roll call.

"Bringing in the Sheaves" didn't help, either. It made her back hurt to think of carrying sheaves.

"May as well put wood in the stove again, as long as I'm awake," she told herself.

Emma was barely out of bed when the shivering be-gan. Quickly she piled wood on the glowing coals and hobbled back to bed, wishing she didn't have to move again for hours and hours. She longed to sink into the cozy depths of sleep—down, down where pain couldn't find her.

"Sing another song," she ordered herself. "'Abide with me, fast falls the ev-en-tide. The dark-ness deepens; Lord, with me abide.' O Lord, I'm so lonesome. It's so dark. I'm scared," she sobbed.

Suddenly, there was Kate! She had burst in the door wearing one of her cotton house dresses, and the light was shining on her hair as it had that day in Phillips. "Emma-lass?" her voice rang out. "Where are you? Heard you cryin'. There be trouble?"

With all the energy she possessed, Emma tried to call out, "I'm here! I'm here in the bedroom!" but no sound came. *I've got to get up! Kate will go away if I don't get out there!* Pain!

Emma jerked awake. All was dark. There was no Kate.

"Kate . . . Kate . . ." she whispered. "What I wouldn't give to have that dream come true! Oh, Kate, I miss you so much!"

The baby gave a little I'm-getting-hungry cry and was quiet again. What time was it? Emma listened intently. She heard the clock's tick, tick, tick—the children's soft breathing—but *no fire snapping!*

"Not again!" she groaned and hoisted herself out of bed.

Not one living coal remained.

Shivering so violently she could scarcely hold the poker, Emma shook down the ashes, crumpled more precious paper, and added more of the meager kindling supply.

While the kindling caught fire, she limped back to the bed, grabbed a comforter and wrapped it around herself.

The baby let out a loud cry. Emma gathered him up and began to nurse him as she stood by the stove, waiting to add more wood.

She anticipated the usual tingle as the milk let down when the baby began to nurse. It didn't come. He nursed a moment and then pulled away and cried.

"*Liebchen . . . Liebchen . . .* Mama's sorry!" Under her

breath Emma scolded herself. "Should have eaten last night, or at least should have drunk more."

With the baby on her shoulder, she poured a cup of water from the teakettle and drank it without stopping. At least it wasn't ice cold.

She put the wood in the stove and took the crying baby to bed with her. When she offered him the other breast, he nursed and dozed.

O Lord . . . thank you! Please keep him sleeping!

Hardly daring to breathe lest she wake him, she gradually relaxed—jaws . . . shoulders . . . arms.

"You must rest," she instructed herself. She wished she had water within her reach. Her body, she knew, needed water—and food—but rest, she decided, was most important.

Father, I thought I had asked You for just about everything. But now I come to You with one more need. Please help my body make the milk my baby has to have.

Rest. Rest.

The clock bonged six.

"Not already!" Emma whispered as she eased the baby into his cradle with another prayer that he would sleep until she had finished the chores.

The cabin was still far from warm as she dressed her shivering body, put more wood in the stove, and drank more water. Had she been less intent on getting the chores done, she might have cried with the pain that stabbed through her with each movement.

Daylight was still far away, and the lantern sat in the barn. Carrying water for the chickens in her right hand and wooden matches in her left, she felt her way to the barn, guided by the high snowbanks on either side of the path. Although she groaned with pain, her legs didn't buckle under her as they had last night. She didn't even spill the water.

She wanted to rush through the chores and get back

to the house, but she held herself back, knowing she must use as little energy as possible so her body could produce milk. The baby wouldn't sleep long, she knew. She wondered what little Albert would do if George cried and cried. Even though she had told him never to take the baby out of the cradle, would he try? Maybe drop him?

She wasted no time feeding the chickens and cattle. Then, warily, she approached Cora. Her knees trembled and pain made her eyes tear, but she managed to hold the pail.

With a firm grip on the milk pail, Emma made her painful way back to the house. Silence greeted her. "O Lord! Thank you! I'm so glad they're still sleeping," she whispered as she took off her coat.

When she had pulled off her overshoes and washed her hands, she poured a cup of warm foamy milk. She hated warm milk, but she took a deep breath and drank it all. She shuddered and wiped her mouth with the back of her hand, willing that milk to go directly where it was needed. Now, if she could just get a little more rest. . . .

Quietly, she put wood in the stove, stirred oatmeal into boiling water, and set the pot on the right-hand lid to simmer. Soundlessly, she crept into bed.

She hadn't even pulled up the comforter when Ellie called, "Mama?"

Emma choked back a groan and whispered, "Come here, *Liebchen.*"

"Go potty first," Emma whispered, when Ellie started to crawl into bed. "Pull your nightie way up! You can do it. You're a big girl. Then you can come and cuddle in with Mama."

Emma held her breath. Would Ellie bang the lid and wake the boys?

"Good girl! Mama's big girl," Emma crooned into Ellie's soft curls when she had snuggled in beside her. She let her breath out slowly, and the quiet settled around her.

Oh, Al! If you only knew . . . you'd come home. I know you would.

Being alone hadn't sounded scary back in Phillips. After living in the clatter and racket of the city, the quiet country had sounded like a haven. She hadn't even thought about trouble, only about the hard work—and that she was willing to face.

Although she knew that Al would have to go to the lumber camp in winter, she had pictured them working *together* year in and year out. "Come help me, Em!" he would say, and she'd give him a hand at whatever the task happened to be. With his strength, skill, and knowledge and her devotion, diligence, and compassion, they would build a home, raise a nice big family, and be happy. There would be laughter and fun and music when the work was done—and love. She smiled to herself. As hard as Al worked, he was seldom too tired for love.

Emma turned on her side and tried to pretend Al's arm was around her and her head was lying on his shoulder. When he held her close like that, she felt as though she was absorbing his strength, his faith, his hopes for the future. In her contentment, her sense of completeness, she'd forget for a while that anything existed but the two of them—until a little one cried.

What if Al hadn't been attracted to her? She never ceased to marvel that he had chosen her. She remembered the first time he had come to her house, to talk to her father with several other surveyors. He hadn't been in the house ten minutes before she knew he was different from the ordinary run of lumberjacks. He laughed and bantered, but she didn't hear a profane word out of him.

Where, she wondered, had she seen him before? Then she recalled. Several years earlier she had been al-

lowed to go with her older sisters on a hayride, and Al
had been along. He had played the accordion and sang.
She didn't know where he had come from, or where he
had gone afterward. In the north woods, many men
came and went.

That day at her folks' home, he didn't speak to her directly. She wasn't certain that he was even aware of her,
yet she thought she felt his eyes follow her as she helped
her mother cook supper. It was like she was seeing herself working, and she was conscious of every move. She
wished she were graceful and beautiful, with wavy black
hair and big brown eyes, instead of straight brown hair
and plain old average-size blue eyes.

At least she wasn't ugly. She'd heard Pa say to Ma
one night, when they thought she had gone up to bed,
that Emma was getting to be a real pretty girl. When Ma
agreed, Emma's eyes filled with tears. Ma wasn't one to
compliment her children, for fear they'd get prideful.
And once her friend Hattie had said she wished she had
a nose like Emma's, so she knew her nose must be all
right. And one time her older brother, Fred, had said
his girl had a complexion almost as clear as Emma's. So
whenever she was getting ready to go out to a gathering,
she'd pull these comforting thoughts out of her memory bank to bolster her confidence.

Emma recalled how she had joined Ma in the front
room with her knitting that night, after the dishes were
done, and stole glances at the men as they talked at the
kitchen table.

"The tallest one," Ma whispered, "That's Al Verleger.
I've heard some good talk about him. He's no ordinary
man. You take notice of him, girl."

Take notice she did. Glancing up from her knitting,
she had managed to record a whole catalogue of de-
tails—the deep dimple in his chin, arms too long for his
shirt, his hearty but not boisterous laugh, his air of confidence in who he was and where he was headed. *Al*

Verleger. So that's who he is.

She told her mother where she had seen him before, on the hayride. "When we got to the top of the Marheine hill and stopped to let the oxen rest, he pulled out his accordion and played and sang. One song I never forgot—'The Maple on the Hill.' I wonder where he's been since then."

"I heard he's been working with the surveyors down around Tomahawk in the summer and in the logging camp in winter."

He had left that day without so much as a glance in her direction, and Emma didn't see him again for several months—not until just before that awful square dance.

The baby stirred and whimpered, and Emma scooped him out of the cradle before he could disturb the other children.

Got to stop daydreaming and think about what's ahead of me today.

Three

The Empty Road

Emma perched precariously on the edge of the chair, keeping the weight off her spine, and ate her oatmeal with the children. She tried to see the snow-covered road out of the window—the frost had melted a few inches.

It was rare that anyone used the road, especially with all the men in the lumber camp for the winter. It wasn't likely Grandpa would come today. He never came two days in a row. But surely someone else would come. Maybe Clara Geber would walk over, as she often did in summer, Emma mused, but then—Clara was fourteen now and worked like a grown woman. Her mother would hardly let her go gadding off on a busy weekday.

Little Fred bounced on the bench behind the table. "Papa's coming home today!" he told Ellie.

"Papa! Papa!" Ellie squealed, waving a spoonful of oatmeal.

Before Emma could catch her hand, the sticky gob landed on Fred's head. He reached up and got it on his hand and let out a wail.

Jaws clenched, Emma hobbled to the washstand for a cloth. "No, Papa's not coming home today," she told Fred as she wiped the oatmeal out of his hair.

Fred wailed louder, and Albert gave him a shove. "Crybaby! He'll be home tomorrow."

Emma ignored their shoving and kicking. *I'll have to get diapers washed today,* she told herself. *Can't wait for someone to come and carry water. Maybe I could let the boys carry in snow to melt for wash water.* "Boys! Stop fighting! I've got an idea."

Albert listened, but Fred kept poking him with his elbow.

"Do you know what happens when you put a tub of snow on the stove?"

They shook their heads.

"It makes water! Let's make a whole tub of water! You can help me."

Albert and Fred looked puzzled.

"You boys can carry in pails and pails of snow, and we'll see how much water it will make. Hurry up and finish eating now!"

Ellie waved her spoon again. "Baby cwy!"

Emma sighed. "I know, I know." She had nursed George while the boys were dressing, but she knew he was still hungry.

"Albert," she called as she picked up the baby, "help Fred with his overshoes when you're done eating, so I can feed the baby."

While Emma nursed the baby, Ellie hung on her knees and cried to go out, too.

"No, *Liebchen*. You stay in and help Mama."

After the first two loads there was only a scant inch of water in the tub, and the door was open so much Emma had to put a coat on Ellie and more wood in the stove.

I should have just gone after a couple pails of water myself, she thought. But even walking on the level floor, she winced with every step, catching her breath at each stab of pain. How would she be able to carry water pails over that slippery, bumpy path?

She peered into the water pail on the bench. With care there would be enough water for drinking and cooking until tomorrow.

After the third load, Albert slumped on a chair. "We're tired."

"Oh, we need lots more!" Emma said. She let him climb on a chair to see into the tub. "Look how little there is."

"All right," he grumbled, and dragged Fred out with him again.

Emma dumped their next loads and handed them the pails again.

Albert set his down. "It's no fun," he pouted.

"No fun," Fred echoed.

"Tell you what," she said cheerily. "I'll help you." She pulled on her coat and grabbed her largest kettle. Glancing hopefully toward the road, she scooped the kettle full of snow. The boys filled theirs, too. Twice more they carried in heaping loads of snow.

Albert heard her groan as she dumped his pailful. "Mama? Is your back hurting?"

She bit her lip and nodded.

"Come on!" he urged Fred. "We've gotta help Mama, 'cause her back hurts." Albert's sympathy lasted through two more loads.

After Emma let them climb on a chair—Ellie, too—to see how much water there was, the boys carried in one more load.

"Aw, Mama, can we quit now?" Albert begged.

Emma sighed. *I'll have to make it do*, she decided. *'ll wash just enough diapers to get through another day or two.* She hugged one boy with each arm and thanked them. "Now you can run and play until you get cold. Maybe you'll find rabbit tracks."

"Or deer tracks!" Albert yelled on his way out the door.

Grateful that Ellie was content to watch them from

the window, Emma stretched out on the bed while the water heated. "Rest!" she ordered her body and proceeded to relax, muscle by muscle. But when she thought about watering the cattle at noon, her body tensed again. How could she make it down that hill and back? How could she haul those buckets of water up out of the river? The ice was so thick she had to get down on her knees and lean way over to lower the bucket.

"Oh, please, Lord, send someone to help me," she pleaded.

Again she tried to let her arms and legs go limp. She imagined her breasts filling, filling with good, warm milk for her baby. . . .

Suddenly Ellie screamed, and Emma lunged out of bed. There was blood running down Ellie's little chin. The last Emma knew, the child had been standing on a chair, watching the boys. She must have slipped and bitten her lip when her chin hit the window sill.

Emma grabbed a little snow from the tub and pressed it against Ellie's lip, assuring her it would stop hurting soon, but Ellie wanted to be rocked. Emma tried to rock her without leaning back, but Ellie wasn't happy in that position. She cried until the boys came in.

Albert couldn't get Fred's overshoes off, so Emma had to tug at them.

The clock struck ten. Tears sprang to Emma's eyes. All those hours yet ahead. . . .

Careful not to spill a drop, Emma poured a little of the water into a washtub to rinse out the diapers. Nose wrinkled as she worked, she wrung them in tight little twists. She poured the dirty water into the slop pail, filling it. She'd have to carry it out. Thankful that the children were playing contentedly, she pulled on her coat, carried out the slop pail, and threw the water down the hillside near the house. Usually she walked all the way to a spot down by the outhouse; she'd have to carry the pot way down there later, she reminded herself.

The worst part of this hurt spine, she decided, was never knowing when or where the next pain would shoot. Now and then she could take a step without hurting, but suddenly a sharp pain would grip so hard that one or both of her legs would buckle under her.

Back in the house she dipped hot water into the tub, saving most of it for rinsing. *I'll only use a little soap,* she thought. *That will be better than not getting all the soap rinsed out—and I'll boil them real good, too.* She had rubbed only two diapers on the washboard when the baby started to cry.

"Albert! Rock the cradle. Mama's got to get these diapers washed."

But the baby kept crying and Albert yelled, "Mama! He won't stop!"

"Oh, dear," Emma muttered as she dried her hands. "Maybe he'll look around a little and be quiet." She took George out of the cradle and set him in the rocking chair. "Albert, hold your hand here on his tummy while I tie him in." She grabbed a strip of old blanket she had often used for this very purpose when the other three were little, and tied it under George's arms and around the back of the chair. "There, now. Rock him gently and talk to him."

She went back to scrubbing diapers and smiled over her shoulder at the antics Albert and Fred went through, trying to make the baby laugh.

"Mama! He likes it!" Albert squealed.

But before Emma had finished rinsing the diapers, the baby was crying again. Hurriedly she rinsed the last few and flung them over the rack behind the stove. These would have to be rewashed when she had more water. The rest, which she had already rinsed well, she set on the stove to boil.

"There, there," she crooned as she took the baby out of the chair. "Mama'll feed you again." When he was contentedly nursing, she murmured, "Seems like all I do is feed you." Her milk supply was still meager. *Lord,* she prayed silently, *I"m trying to drink a lot and eat and rest all I can. I can't do anything more. Please help me!*

She toyed with the idea of giving the baby a little cow's milk with a spoon. No, she wouldn't try that. She remembered too well the baby three houses down in Phillips. His mother had tried that, and it had made him terribly sick. If Georgie were a few months older, she would feed him some strained oatmeal, but he wasn't quite three months old. Surely by tomorrow she'd have plenty of milk again.

As she put the baby back in the cradle, she thought about watering the cattle, and a wave of panic washed over her. She would have to do it while Fred and Ellie took their naps—if no one had come by that time.

Emma set the boiling diapers aside to cool and crept back to bed. Nine hours until bedtime. . . . If only she were back in Phillips. She closed her eyes and pictured herself in her little house with Kate right across the street. What would she have done without Kate the time the children had burned with fever for three days and she didn't know what was wrong with them?

She had seen one of the Riley girls outside that cold winter day and called to her that the children were sick. Would she ask her mother to please come over?

Emma smiled as she recalled how quickly Kate had come.

"Albert, let me see your tongue," Kate had said sternly.

He had whined and turned his head away.

"Come, lad," she said in a patient, yet compelling, way. "I need to see it."

Gently she turned his head to the light. "Ah. 'Tis the measles, he has. Another day 'n' they'll be breakin' out, and the fever will go down some."

Kate told her to keep giving them water, little sips real often, and to pull the shades down so the light wouldn't hurt their eyes.

"Pitiful, they are," she said, looking back from the door. "An' I see your black eyes 'n ' my heart aches for ye! But it's courage you'll be needin', not pity, and you'll not be gettin' it from the likes o' me." Then, taking Emma's face between her hands and ignoring Emma's tears, she said, "These days will soon be behind ye. Take one hour. Do all that ye should that hour the very best you can. When the next hour comes, do the same—all the while knowin' God will give you all the strength you'll be needin'."

Emma had nodded then, wiped her tears on her sleeve, and smiled a tiny smile. Now she opened her eyes and stared at the rough log wall. Kate might as well be a thousand miles away, rather than forty. There was no way she could come. Emma turned her face into the pillow so the children wouldn't hear her. "Al . . . how could you leave me like this? How can you go away each Sunday, not knowing what will happen while your gone?" Sobs shook her body. "And even if I get through these days," she continued, "what will I do about all the days after Sunday?"

The clock struck twelve.

"Cryin' won't help," she could hear Kate say. "Soon as a body starts feelin' sorry for herself, it's all downhill."

Emma took a deep breath, struggled out of bed, smoothed her hair, and hobbled to the washtub. She wrung out the diapers, gave each one a smart snap, and hung them on the drying rack.

High time she fed the children, she realized, as Al and Fred began fighting and Ellie ran and clung to her skirt. She scrambled eggs, sliced bread (she'd have to bake tomorrow), and poured milk. She tied a dish towel around Ellie's neck and took another look up the road.

The children were curious and craned their necks in the direction of her gaze.

"The chickadees are looking for bread crumbs. I forgot to put some out," she explained. "Here, Albert, put these way up on the snowdrift—as high as you can reach—so we can watch from the window."

Albert came in shivering. "Mama? Don't their feet get cold?"

"I guess not. They don't seem to mind the cold snow."

"Wish I had feet like theirs," Albert mumbled.

"Where do the birds sleep, Mama?" asked Fred.

Emma told him they had nests somewhere in the trees. All the while she kept glancing toward the road. *Now Lord!* she prayed silently. *Have someone come now!*

Ellie yawned. Nap time. Emma decided to let the children stay up while she washed the dishes, but she soon regretted it. Ellie whined, and Fred and Albert squabbled.

When the younger children were asleep, Emma stood for another moment staring up the road. Then, with a sigh, she took a piece of brown wrapping paper and a pencil from the clock shelf. "I'll sharpen the pencil for you, and you can draw pictures while I'm outside," she told Albert.

As she sharpened the pencil over the open stove lid, she still hoped to look up and see a dark figure coming down the road.

Albert chattered happily. "I'll draw trees . . . and rabbits . . . and deers."

One more look. Emma took her coat off the hook. "Don't take the baby out of the cradle. And if Fred and Ellie wake up, don't let 'em climb on anything—"

"I know, Mama. You *always* say that!" Albert said with an exasperated sigh. He set to work drawing.

Tears of disappointment brimmed in her eyes as Emma carried the pot out with her. She left it by the path while she let out the ox and the cows. No need to chase the thirsty animals to the river. They headed for the water hole the minute she untied them.

She dumped the pot and took time to use the outhouse before she went on down to the river to water the livestock. She had to crawl under the fence Al had put around the hole in the river ice and then get down on her knees.

Her knees! Emma had forgotten her cut knees. She tried to pad them with her coat, but they still hurt as she plunged the bucket into the icy water and pulled it up by the rope tied to the handle. She shoved the first bucket under the fence to the ox. Once he had his fill, the cows would have room.

By the time she had hoisted up the third bucket, searing pain was shooting up her back and down her legs. She knew how important the water was to the cattle, but her knowledge didn't ease the pain a bit.

When they had finally drunk their fill, Emma rolled over onto her right hip and rested a moment before getting up. "Lord, I don't understand," she said out loud, her breath making white clouds around her. "You know how much this hurts. Why didn't you send someone to help me?" She wiped tears on her rough sleeve and struggled to her feet. She cried out her disappointment on the way back to the house, but stopped before she opened the door to compose her face.

When she stepped in the door, Albert ran to her, picture in hand. "Mama? Are you cryin'?"

She evaded his question. "Well, now! Let's see what you drew." She tried to concentrate on his lengthy explanation as she yanked off her overshoes. "Tell you what," she said, "let's you and I lie down, and I'll tell you a story."

Albert's eyes sparkled as he hopped up on the bed.

Very carefully, lest she cry out, Emma stretched out beside him. Pain engulfed her, and she patted Albert's back until she could trust herself to speak. "Let's see.

Once upon a time. . .there was a little boy, and he. . . and he. . . ." A spasm of shivers shook her.

Albert patted her cheek. "Mama? You want me to tell *you* a story?"

Emma sighed. "That would be nice. You tell me a story."

He wiggled his arms out from the covers. "Uh. Once there was a little boy, 'n' his Papa bought him a b-i-g ax." He stretched his arms to show how big it was, bumping Emma in the nose. "An' his Papa took him along to camp. . . ."

Emma murmured appropriate sounds as Albert talked and talked.

When he stopped, she said, "That was a nice story," but Albert didn't respond. He was asleep. Smiling, Emma eased the covers up to his dimpled chin—a miniature of Al's.

How often she had thought of Al's deep-dimpled chin those weeks after his first visit to their house. For a while, she had no idea where he was until she heard her father tell her mother that Siegfried Verleger was home-steading a few miles south, and his son Albert had filed claim to the adjoining quarter section.

Then one July day, right after a thundershower, there had been a knock on the door. There stood Al, smiling down at her.

"Pa's not home," she said quickly, feeling her face flush, "and Ma's down with a sick headache, and the baby's sleeping, so I can't ask you in."

"The baby?"

Emma nodded. "My sister Anne died in May. Ma and Pa took little Anne."

"Oh, yes. I remember hearing about your sister. I'm sorry. I didn't know her baby was here. Uh . . . mind if I sit here on the steps in the sun and dry out a bit? Got caught in that shower."

She had hesitated at the door, not knowing if she

should join him. Then he said, "Got time to sit and talk awhile?" He cleared his throat. "I didn't come to see your father. I . . . I came to see you."

"You did?" she exclaimed, and immediately wished she could take back the words which had betrayed her delight. She sat down several feet from him.

"The air smells good after the rain," he commented.

She murmured agreement and added, "I like the brick color of the ground while it's still wet."

"Down where I come from, we have dark brown soil. It still surprises me to see things grow so well in this red clay."

"Where do you come from?"

"Wind Lake, near Hale's Corners—not too far from Milwaukee."

"I was born in Oshkosh. We came up here when I was ten."

"Ever wish you were back in the city?"

"Sometimes. It gets lonesome here. But I like the country better than the city," she added quickly.

"Then you're not planning to run off to the city like a lot of girls do."

She laughed and shook her head. "My sister Gustie used to work for some real rich people in Milwaukee. She used to tell us what it was like. I don't think I'd like it. Anyway, Ma needs me now that the baby is here."

They talked on about many things until Emma heard the baby cry. She brought her out in the sunshine. When little Anne smiled at Al, he reached out his arms for her. For a few moments he talked to the baby as though he had forgotten Emma was even there. He sang a silly little song and bounced the baby his knee. He grinned at Emma. "I hope I have about a dozen kids."

"Me, too," Emma agreed. "I can't imagine how anyone could not like babies. My mother always says not to trust anyone who doesn't like babies and flowers."

Al smiled. "I'll have to remember that." He pulled

his watch out of his vest pocket and stood up. "Gotta get goin'. Pa'll be waiting for me. Hey! Would you like to go to the square dance at the schoolhouse Saturday night?"

Of course Emma had said yes, though she hated square dancing.

Albert rolled over, bringing Emma's thoughts abruptly back to the present. She smiled. Well, they certainly had a good start toward those dozen children.

Four

Strength for Each Task

From far down in the dark depths of slumber, Emma heard the baby cry. She struggled to open her eyes, but they were glued shut and her body anchored to the bed. . . . For what seemed like hours she tried to move, until her right leg jerked and pain streaked along her nerves. Her eyes flew open.

Morning? No. She was wearing her clothes. Now she remembered. She had watered the stock, and then had lain down to rest with Albert.

Both the baby and the fire needed tending. Emma rolled out of bed and gasped as pain held her in its grip.

"Oh, dear," she muttered. "Watering the stock didn't do me any good." She grasped the back of a chair for support. Before she got to the stove, the three little ones were clamoring at her feet.

Albert grinned up at her. "I woke up, but you still kept sleeping."

"You sleeped long," Fred chided, as though she had forsaken them.

"I took care of 'em real good, Mama!" Albert said, nodding his head. "You gonna tell Papa?"

"That I will," she promised him as she shoved wood in the stove, grateful for a bed of hot coals.

While Ellie begged to be held, Emma stole a glance at the clock. "Oh dear," she said, "It's nearly three." Emma put a hand on Ellie's soft curls and asked, "Want to cuddle in bed with me while I feed baby George?"

Ellie beat her to the bed.

"Boys!" Emma called when the baby had quieted. "I forgot to gather the eggs. You want to do it?"

They ran for their coats.

"Be sure you swing the bar all the way over," she warned, "so you don't get locked in if the door slams shut."

When they were finally dressed and out the door, Emma tried to let her body go slack, but the nagging pain kept her taut.

Ellie soon grew dissatisfied with Emma's brief answers to her chatter, and crawled out of bed to run to the window. "Go out! Go out!" she wailed. She charged back to the bed and lunged against it.

Emma cried out, and Ellie stopped, wide-eyed.

"You're just a little girl," Emma explained when she had caught her breath. "You have to grow bigger, and then you can go out with the boys."

"Big dirl! Big dirl!" Ellie insisted, tears dripping down her cheeks.

"I know what!" Emma said brightly. "Wait just a minute." She rolled the baby to the center of the bed, got up, and hobbled to the pantry. "Sit down at the table," she called to Ellie. "I'm bringing you a surprise."

Ellie wriggled on her tummy, trying to crawl up on a chair, as Emma put a handful of raisins on the table.

"Eat 'em one at a time, *Liebchen*," she said, giving her a quick hug.

Once more Emma eased herself back in bed with the still hungry baby and tried to relax. She smoothed his soft hair with her forefinger. "Drink all there is," she crooned. "Mama will feed you often." *I must remember to take a big drink when I get up*, she reminded herself.

If she could keep the baby satisfied one more day, surely her milk supply would catch up when Al did the chores Saturday night and Sunday morning. But what about all the days *after* Sunday? The familiar knot of fear tightened its grip, and Emma groaned so loud Ellie heard her.

"Mama?"

"It's all right. Eat your raisins now."

"All gone," Ellie announced, running to the bed and bouncing against it again.

Emma winced. "Oh! I hear the boys. Go see!"

They tramped in, white with snow.

"Shake your coats by the door—no, wait. Albert, come here."

She took a square of soft cloth from under her pillow and wiped his nose before she said, "I need a piece of venison from the woodshed. Think you can reach it if you stand on the splitting block?"

His eyes brightened. "Sure I can!"

He ran off, Fred right behind him. "No! Fred, you stay here. Albert will be right back. He's just going to get some meat."

Reluctantly, Fred shed his coat, but he couldn't get his overshoes off and started to cry. Ellie wailed at the window again, wanting to go out.

Emma sighed. At least the baby wasn't crying.

She tended the fire again, pulled off Fred's overshoes, and limped over to comfort Ellie.

"Oh, my! Look how it's snowing. Good thing it's snowing today, instead of tomorrow when Papa walks home from Ogema."

Ellie stopped crying.

"Papa? Papa?"

"Not now! *Tomorrow* he'll come home." Emma

shook her head. How did one explain "tomorrow" to a seventeen-month-old?

Fred snuggled against her. He asked, "Mama? What's a Ogema?"

"Ogema is a town. Papa will ride the train in to Ogema from the camp and walk home from there."

"What's a train?"

"A train is . . . well, it's something people ride on, and it hauls logs and things. It has a big black engine and goes 'Woo! Woo!'"

Fred liked that. He ran around the rocker, crying, "Woo! Woo!" and Ellie chased after him.

The baby started to cry, and Emma picked him up and held him close. *Lord, I don't want these little ones to grow up never even seeing a town or a train or stores or people. We need those horses! But how am I going to keep going alone?*

She changed the baby, laid him down, and tried to think about supper. Surveying her meager supplies, she decided on potato soup. Her aching body yearned for the bed, but a glance at the clock told her it was time to peel potatoes.

Albert must be having trouble reaching the meat, she thought, as she dug out wrinkled potatoes and broke off the white sprouts. She peeled them, put them in a pot with barely enough water to cover them, and set the potatoes to boil.

"Where is that boy?" Emma muttered, looking out into the snow-covered back yard. "I should have told him not to play. It's getting dark." She put wood in the stove again and looked out the window, wishing the shed door faced the east so she could see it.

Ellie was running in circles, with Fred in pursuit, and bumped her head on the table. Emma kissed the hurt.

"Fred! Stop it now. You're getting too wild."

He made one more circle, ending at the window. "Albert ain't comin' wight back," he pouted.

"He'll be coming in a minute," she assured him. "You watch for him."

Emma opened the door, and a swirl of snow blew through the lean-to and into the house. "Albert!" she called. She listened for an answer but heard nothing but howling wind. No use yelling.

She set soup bowls on the table, added milk and butter to the potatoes, and went to the window. Still no Albert. Maybe he had fallen trying to get the meat down. The baby began to cry, and Emma rocked his cradle. "I can't stop to feed you again right now. Go to sleep!"

Emma knew what she had to do. Balancing on the edge of a chair, she pulled on her overshoes.

"Fred, come here," she said, trying to keep her voice calm. She pulled on her coat as she instructed him to rock the cradle but not *ever* to take the baby out.

"An' don't let Ellie climb on *anything!*" he added.

"That's right," she said, hiding a brief smile. "Watch me from the window."

Heart thumping, she shuffled through the soft snow, imagining Albert in a crumpled heap, an arm or leg broken. *Oh Lord! Don't let him be hurt!* She could see that the shed door was shut, the bar in place. "Albert! Where are you?" she called.

"In here!" a little voice answered through the wailing wind.

She swung the bar up and to the left and yanked open the door.

Albert sat huddled on the splitting block, his head pulled into his coat like a little turtle. Stiffly he toddled toward her, dragging the meat in its flour sack.

"The bar musta fallen down," he said through chattering teeth. "I got the meat," he added proudly.

Emma held him close, not mentioning the tear tracks on his cheeks. "Thank God, you're all right! Next time be sure the bar's way over," she warned. She ushered him ahead of her. "Run on now. I'll be right with you."

As she made her way slowly back to the house, Emma thought how much worse things could be if Albert had fallen and hurt himself. When she got inside, she pulled heavy woolen socks on his icy, white feet. At first they were numb, and she urged him to walk to get the blood circulating in them.

Even though she warned him that they would hurt when the blood began to move, the little boy wasn't prepared for such severe pain. He cried. He howled. He wailed. Fred and Ellie cried too, simply because Albert was crying, and Emma felt ready to sit down and bawl with them.

She poured the soup in bowls and urged Albert to come and eat, but he sat on the rug in front of the stove, holding his feet and rocking in pain.

Fred and Ellie didn't have to be coaxed. Before they finished their soup, hunger drove Albert, still sniffling, to the table. He took a spoonful of soup, choked, and cried again, clutching his feet.

"There, there. The hurt will stop real soon now," Emma assured him. But her heart ached as she thought about the chilblains he would suffer. She could hardly remember a winter when she *hadn't* had chilblains. The red, sore areas on her feet itched and hurt at the same time. Sometimes she rubbed them with a freshly cut raw potato, easing the itching and pain a bit.

But frost-bitten feet, she realized, were nothing compared to a broken limb. What would she have done if he had broken a bone? That was another question to add to her list for Al when he got home.

After she cleared the table, she lit the lamp in the wall bracket. Three little faces turned to her, knowing she was getting ready to leave them. As she reached for her coat she began the usual warning: "Don't climb on *anything . . . .* "

She sighed. They were already at play, chattering

among themselves, not paying a bit of attention to her warning. "Lord," she whispered as she pulled on her coat, "keep them safe."

As she poured precious hot water into a pail for the chickens, the thought came to her: *Let them look at the mail order catalog.*

For a moment she argued with herself. Should she risk having them tear it? Would Al be angry if they did? She wished she had the old one, but it was fast growing slim in the outhouse.

She hobbled to the pantry and took the book from the top shelf. "*Kinder!*" she called, "If you promise to be *very* careful, I'll let you look at the catalog while I do chores."

"We will! We will!" Albert and Fred chimed as they scrambled up on the bench behind the table.

"Don't take it off the table—and let Ellie see it, too."

Closing the door softly behind her, Emma headed into the white whirling world. A misstep sent a jab of pain up her spine. She clenched her teeth and stumbled on. At one spot a drift was deeper than her shoe-tops, and she felt an icy ring around each leg. Suddenly a gust of wind threw her off balance, and she landed with her right arm up to the elbow in snow. The pail with the water for the chickens lay on its side.

She was about to cry over the spilled water when a new fear gripped her—what if the storm got so bad that Al couldn't get home tomorrow?

"Lord! Stop the storm! Please stop it!" Emma sobbed as she fought her way into the barn. She shook so violently she had to use three matches to light the lantern. Instead of dragging hay to the ox and cows, she stumbled toward patient Molly and flung herself over Molly's warm back.

"I can't," she sobbed. "I just can't do it!"

A shred of memory stirred. There was another time she had sobbed, "I just can't do it!" She could see it plainly in her mind—the vegetable cart and the muddy road in Oshkosh, when she was about nine.

Walter and Winnie had told her to take the vegetables up the hill to Rommel's boarding house, while they took baskets to other customers down near the lake. She had done it before, when the road was hard and dry, but on this particular day the road was oozing with mud. The mud lodged between the spokes of the wheels and, before she was halfway up the hill, the cart was stuck fast.

Emma had pushed and pulled and prayed, "God, send someone to help me!" When no one came she had bawled and sobbed, "Lord, I can't. I just can't do it!"

She was about to leave the cart when she remembered some words she had heard often in their little church: "I can do all things through Christ which strengthens me."

As she began to repeat it, she *knew* the cart would move. And it had. Slowly, slowly she had made her way to Rommel's and delivered the vegetables.

Molly shifted under her weight. Feeling calmer now, Emma began to drag hay to the cattle. She remembered how she had run to tell Ma about her triumph with the cart, but Ma hadn't been pleased. In fact, she had scolded Emma for trying to use God's Word like magic. And Emma hadn't tried ever again—until now.

Why were we given God's Word, she argued with herself, *if we aren't supposed to use it?* She thought about it all the while she fed the cattle. As she sat down gingerly to milk Cora, the thought came to her that surely, if she were facing something she *had* to do, but couldn't do in her own strength, she could count on God's strength.

"Of course!" she said out loud. "Ma was afraid I might try to do foolish, impossible things—things I had no business doing."

Father, she prayed as she struggled to hold the pail,

which was steadily growing heavier, *St. Paul said he could do all things—all the things he had to do—through Christ's strength. Help me do that now. Thank you for reminding me of how you helped me years ago.*

As she got up from milking Cora, faith welled up within her. All the way from the barn to the house, with the snow swirling around her and pain searing through her, Emma repeated that comforting verse.

Before she opened the door she could hear them: Ellie squealing, the baby crying, and the boys yelling.

"Oh, no!" She groaned at the sight of Ellie, sitting with the catalog across her knees, gleefully tearing out pages.

Ellie's delighted squeals abruptly turned to frustrated wails as Emma rescued the catalog.

"Boys! Stop fighting!" she yelled at the miniature wrestlers, who were rolling dangerously close to the stove. They were still at it when she had taken off her coat and overshoes. Pain shooting up her spine and down her legs, Emma grabbed one boy in each hand, shook them, and ordered them to sit in opposite corners.

Reluctantly they obeyed, still yelling, "He wouldn't let me—" and "It was my turn—."

With a crying babe on her shoulder and Ellie clinging to her skirt, Emma fought the desire to scream. She wanted to lay the baby back down, pry Ellie's hands from her skirt, and run out into the night. Her legs trembled and threatened to give way. She had a sudden vision of herself, coatless, running into the storm, with the children screaming after her.

"Lord! Help me!" she pleaded out loud. What were those words she was going to remember—the ones she had said all the way to the house? At least she could quiet the baby, and she unbuttoned her dress front.

Heart pounding, trembling with pain, she tried to soothe Ellie. "*Liebchen!* Listen to Mama! Papa's coming home tomorrow."

Ellie ran to the window.

"No, no! Not now! Tomorrow! After you sleep."

After the boys assured her there would be no more fighting, she asked them to try to explain to Ellie when Papa was coming home and promised them bread and syrup with their milk as soon as she put the baby down.

She wasn't prepared for the stab of pain when she tried to stand up, and almost lost her balance. Teeth clenched, she poured milk and spread bread with syrup.

Fred bumped Albert's arm, spilling most of Albert's milk. While Emma wiped it up, Ellie laid her arm on her syrup bread and wailed because she was sticky.

From then until they were in bed, the children balked continually whenever Emma told them to do something. She was on the verge of spanking all three of them, but held herself back lest she spank much too hard. When they were finally quiet she stood, fingers pressed against her temples, and tried to think what she had to do before she could crawl into bed.

She carried more wood in from the lean-to, filled the stove, and closed the draft almost all the way. She braided her hair and drank another cup of milk.

In bed, Emma let out her breath jerkily as waves of pain swept through her. *Lord, please ease the pain. Help me sleep and please, oh please, make the storm stop.*

Five

Memories in the Night

It seemed to Emma that she had hardly fallen to sleep when the baby cried. It was no surprise; he needed much more milk than she had supplied today. Fearful of nursing him in bed, lest she fall asleep and smother him, she pulled the rocker closer to the stove and sat there with a comforter tucked around them both.

There was so much she should do tomorrow. She always scrubbed the pine floorboards with lye soap the day before Al came home. Not this week, she decided. She'd have all she could do to carry water, feed the children, do morning chores, and water the cattle at noon. And there was the bread to bake, and—"Oh my goodness!" she whispered. "I forgot to set the yeast. I'll do it as soon as I put the baby down."

All those long hours ahead of her. What was it Kate had said? "Take one hour at a time. Do the best you can that hour."

"Oh, Kate!" Emma whispered. "I'll try. But I sure wish you were here to help me!"

Before she shifted George to the other breast, Emma leaned over and opened the draft. The baby protested with a sharp cry.

"Oh, *Liebchen*, you think you have troubles," she whispered. "I wish I were little again."

She wiggled into a more comfortable position, letting her thoughts take her back in time. She could see the streets in Oshkosh from her early childhood. She recalled how strange the board sidewalks of Ogema seemed that day she and Mama and the other children arrived by train, leaving Oshkosh behind.

Poor Papa! He had met them at the train and tried to lift her down, but she wouldn't let him because she didn't know him with a beard! He'd been gone a year, working in the Northern Wisconsin pine forests so far from his family. He must have been so lonely, she realized now.

The board sidewalks were soon left behind as they walked through what seemed to be endless woods. Ten long miles they had hiked, taking two days to do it. She'd never forget seeing that little log cabin by the creek for the first time. It was like living in a storybook.

How many times she had walked that ten miles since—including the day of her wedding, when she walked with her right hand in Al's, her left hand fingering the smooth poplin of her silvery-gray wedding dress.

Ma would have frowned and scolded, had she seen Emma fingering her dress like that. "You look like a baby doing that—like you're still dragging your baby quilt around. You used to feel its edge till you were three. Then when you let go that quilt, you'd be sittin' there fingering your skirt every time I looked at you."

It was an odd habit. Emma wasn't usually aware she was doing it till Ma scolded or her brothers teased. That thought took her back to the night of the square dance. She was sitting, watching the dancers and feeling the calico material of her skirt slide through her fingers, when nine-year-old Dick ran past and yelled, "Want your blanket, baby?"

Probably no one else had heard him, but her face flamed. *I never should have told Al I'd come. I can't dance.*

The last time she'd tried, she had made so many wrong turns that Walter and Dick said she looked like a cow trying to find the right stall. This night she felt like all eyes were on her, though she hadn't made quite as many blunders. When she twisted her ankle, she was secretly glad and pretended it hurt more than it really did so she could limp to a seat.

But then she had to sit and watch Millie Luft flashing her big brown eyes at Al as she swooped and twirled, never making one wrong move. Hattie, her best friend, had sat with her a little while but then off she went, whirling as gracefully as Millie, while Emma sat with the old ladies.

Surely Al would sit out one dance and talk with her. She waited and smiled at those around her, and even clapped her hands. But Al just kept on dancing.

When Emma felt like she had been sitting there for hours, Ma came up. "You're riding home with us."

Emma looked pleadingly at Al, and Ma said, "Dick, go tell Al Verleger that Emma's going home."

Al didn't even wave when she hobbled to the door.

Ma had tried to console her when they got home. "He'll come by tomorrow, you'll see." But he hadn't. In fact, it was almost September before she saw him again.

Emma could see that scene in her mind just as plain as if it had been yesterday. There was Al, coming up the lane, his hair blowing in the wind, his coat tail standing straight out behind him. Her first impulse had been to have Ma tell him he could just go see Millie Luft, but she found herself at the door, hoping he couldn't hear how hard her heart was pounding.

When she opened the door, he took her hand and pulled her right out on the stoop. His words tumbled out. "Emma, I wanted to come see you the day after the dance, but I had to help Pa. New families came from Germany, and I've been working and working. . . ."

She squeezed his hand. "You're here now. Want to sit down?"

"Soon as I get a drink," he said, taking the tin cup off the wire hook on the pump. He held the cup in his left hand and pumped with his right—something Emma couldn't do because her arms weren't long enough to reach.

When he sat down, he took her hand again. She didn't want to pull it away, although the thought flitted through her mind that she really ought to. She soaked up his enthusiastic words about the land he had filed a claim on and about the new settlers coming in. It was wonderful to hear what was going on outside her own household. She hoped he wouldn't ask her what had been happening in her life, because nothing had. The only new things she ever saw were what baby Anne learned.

Al stayed for supper that night, but it seemed to Emma that he paid little attention to her. At dusk he said he had to leave and asked Emma to walk to the main road with him. He didn't even hold her hand, she remembered, until they reached the road. Then he gave her hand a quick squeeze and said, "You're gonna be at the box social next week, aren't you?" and he was gone.

She walked back to the house that night in a welter of emotions—miffed because he had talked with the family all evening, disappointed because he hadn't offered to *take* her to the social, and yet thrilled that he had come to see her and was, perhaps, looking forward to seeing her again.

So long ago. . . . Emma held baby George up to her shoulder, kissed the top of his head, and smiled, remembering how excited she had been preparing her lunch and decorating that box for the social.

Ma had helped her cover the box with some material left over from her new skirt. It had looked real pretty when they were done. Ma found some blue yarn that just matched, and Emma tied the box with it and made a bow on the top.

She'd had to wear her old skirt that night, or everyone would know which box was hers. When the bidding started on her box, she could hardly breathe. Big, old, red-faced Gus kept bidding, but so did Al. He hadn't even placed a bid on another box. How did he know it was hers? Or did he?

Al got it for seventy-five cents, one of the highest bids of the evening. He led Emma to a quiet corner of the hall where the girls hung their coats. She took out the napkins and arranged the sandwiches on them. She'd take out the molasses cake later.

"I was wondering how I'd ever know your box, but then I saw your material. You wore that skirt the night I had supper at your house. Emma, I didn't know you were so clever!"

Emma felt her face burn. "I never thought of that, Al, honest! I never thought you'd remember my skirt material."

He gave her a quick, one-armed hug. "Now I can walk you home. I wanted to bring you this evening, but that's not exactly fair at a box social. I might have had to see another girl home, if I'd ended up with her supper!" *What a dummy I was! I was wishing Al would kiss me that night, but still I was scared. Maybe he knew I was scared, and that's why he just hugged me and said it was nice to be with me.*

She smiled into the darkness, thinking how Al's huge frame would fill the doorway tomorrow evening. The little ones would cling to his legs, and he'd wink at her over their clamor. She'd pretend to be busy, but she'd be waiting until the children's excitement had subsided. Then he'd come and wrap her in his long arms. She wouldn't even mind the odor of greasy camp cooking that clung to his woolen shirt, or his week's growth of whiskers. She'd just cling, unaware for a moment of the children, and let all her tension seep into his strong body.

But maybe this time she'd better not cling. How could she possibly— Oh, dear! A week was so long for a man. Would he be angry? Surely he'd realize what she had been through these days. Maybe he'd praise her for struggling so hard.

She imagined Al helping her to bed, insisting that he take over completely so she could rest. He'd shake his head and say, "I don't know how you did it!"

The fire snapped, and the baby started. Emma carefully laid him in his cradle and then got busy setting the yeast and filling the stove. Back in bed, the pain didn't seem so bad when she thought how wonderful if would be just to lie there and rest and rest and rest when Al got home.

The fire snapped. "Ah . . . good!" she whispered and snuggled deeper into the covers, blissfully free of pain for the moment. Now, if the baby would sleep a long while. . . .

A gust of wind shook the windowpanes and howled around the corner of the house, and the baby began to cry in earnest. Once more Emma hauled herself out of bed, pulled on her robe, lined the rocker with a comforter from her bed, and put wood in the stove.

"I wonder what time it is," she said to herself when she was settled with the baby. No matter. The clock would strike soon and she'd know. Emma dozed, till her head fell on her shoulder and woke her.

Now and then the fire snapped and the wind whistled down the chimney. Otherwise all was quiet. Strangely quiet. Suddenly she was alert. Something wasn't right.

She yawned. "I'm half asleep, that's all," she told

herself. But after she had tucked the baby back in the cradle, she realized what was missing. The clock! It wasn't ticking! It hadn't struck once during the time she was up with the baby.

Emma lit a match. In the flame's flare she saw the hands standing at five after twelve. Never in all her married life had she forgotten to wind the clock before she went to bed. How could she have forgotten tonight? Well, there was nothing for it now but to wait until Al was home with his pocket watch and could reset it.

The cold wind, determined to creep into the cabin, found a thousand cracks and crevices. Emma shivered and tucked quilts around the children cuddled in the little bed. When the weather got warm, they would sleep upstairs in the little room Al had lined with boards last summer.

An eerie sound rose above the wind, and Emma tensed. It sounded like wolves. A chill raced up her spine and down her arms. She hadn't heard wolves since they came back from Phillips.

With the comforter wrapped around her, she peered out into the darkness, remembering a winter night when Albert was a baby. Al was away then, too, and those horrible creatures had edged closer and closer to the cabin. Clara Geber was with her that night; she had often stayed over then. If only Clara were with her now.

Emma held her breath and listened again. Nothing but the wind now. Still, she waited by the window. The other time, the wolves had been attracted by their little dog. Poor little fellow. He had huddled against the door, whining and barking as the drooling, snarling beasts closed in on him, but she hadn't dared open the door to let him in.

She had set lamps in the windows, because she remembered Al saying that wolves would never attack a person with a light. Then she had carried Albert up the ladder to the cold loft and tried to keep him from crying until the wolves slunk back to the woods, leaving the little dog trembling pitifully, but unharmed.

It must have been my imagination, Emma assured herself and hobbled back to bed. *How long before daylight?* she wondered, scolding herself over and over for forgetting to wind the clock. How could she have been so careless? Now she would have only daylight to go by. She wouldn't even know when to put the roast in the oven.

Eventually she slept, waking only when the baby cried again. Objects in the room were faintly taking shape. *Must be after six*, she estimated.

There was no water for the chickens, she realized when she was ready to do chores. She'd fill their water dish with snow until she could carry some. Snow pelted Emma's face when she opened the door of the lean-to. Whether it was new snow falling from the sky or just snow being blown about by the raging wind, she didn't know.

She started to ask God to stop the storm, but then stopped. *What's the sense of praying,* she thought. *My prayers don't get answered anyway. But if Al doesn't get home—*

"I won't think about that," Emma said as she yanked the barn door open. "I'll do what I have to do right now—this hour—like Kate said, and then I'll face the next hour."

So far her back didn't hurt as much as yesterday. So far. She rested her head on Molly's warm, sturdy flank as she milked her—as she had rested her head on Al's chest that bright autumn day when they had walked down by the creek and talked about their future. Emma laughed aloud. Al wouldn't be flattered to hear that Molly's flank reminded her of his chest!

He had held her gently in his arms that day—no more one-armed hugs. "You're different from most girls, Emma," he had said.

"In what way?"

"I never felt that I could trust a girl before. I've heard my sisters plan their silly games; 'If you tell him this or that, he'll do thus and so.' You wouldn't do that, would you—try to make me jealous, so I'd pay more attention to you?

Emma had raised her head and looked into his eyes. She wanted to be serious, but she heard herself giggle. "No, I wouldn't. I wouldn't know how!"

Al threw back his head and laughed. "I hope you never learn. You'll be all right, if you stay away from foolish women. Just be yourself."

Then his smile faded, and his eyes held hers. It was as though nothing on earth could keep her from him now. Closer and closer she felt herself being drawn, until his lips were on hers. Those precious lips she could have drawn from memory were on hers, telling her what words couldn't express—and she was saying things right back! It was as though all she had been feeling for him was rising in a huge, glowing ball.

It was all she could do to choke back the words "I love you!" She must wait to hear it from him first. Thinking back now, Emma realized it probably wasn't more than ten seconds before he whispered, "I love you, Emma!" At the time it had seemed more like ten minutes

She thought she should probably hold back, wait until the next time she saw him, before she said the same to him, but the words came from deep within and there was no stopping them.

The next kiss left her head spinning and her knees trembling. She'd never known a person could feel like this. She had leaned against his chest again, and Al had said, "We'd better get back to the house."

Al had gone off to the lumber camp that winter, and she must have relived those moments a thousand times while he was away. So long ago now . . . five, six, no, over seven years ago. Emma shook her head. *And I thought that once we were married, we'd always be together like that.*

What's the matter with me! I'm thinking like a silly schoolgirl.

Emma picked up the full pail of milk and headed back for the house, groaning with each step. Al just had to get home.

Six

Emma's Decision

It wasn't until she was pouring milk for the children's breakfast that Emma glanced over at the window and saw the geranium. She gave a little cry, setting the pitcher down so hard that milk splashed out.

Before she got around the table, she knew the plant was hopelessly frozen, its darkened leaves already drooping. She cradled the limp bud-cluster in her right fingers and wiped her tears with the left.

Albert's head pressed against her hip. "It's only a flower, Mama."

She patted his firm little cheek. "I know . . . but it would have been so pretty."

She felt his head nod. "It'll grow again."

"No. It's frozen too badly. See, the whole stem is clear, like ice." She handed the flower pot to him. "Go set it out in the lean-to. If Grandma gives me another slip, I'll plant it in the same pot."

Emma went to stir the oatmeal, afraid to discover what else she might have forgotten.

"Tell you what, boys," she said, when they were eating breakfast. "When you're done eating, you can carry wood in for the wood box."

"Me too! Me too!" Ellie insisted.

"Well, now, Ellie, why don't you help Mama bake bread?"

"Dough! Dough!" she yelled, waving her spoon.

The last few times Emma had baked bread, she had given Ellie a ball of dough to play with *I wonder how many children I could have*, Emma thought, *before I'd stop being thrilled when they learn something new?*

Of course Ellie wanted the dough *right now*, and pulled at Emma's skirt while she heated milk and mixed it with flour and the yeast mixture. As quickly as she could, Emma worked flour into a portion of dough for Ellie, sifted a bit of flour onto the oilcloth, and gave Ellie her dough. "Close that door as fast as you can," Emma reminded the boys as they dragged wood in and thumped it on the floor.

Time and again her eyes went to the clock. "Never realized how many times a day I look at the clock," she said to herself. "I feel cut off from the whole world, not knowing what time it is." She looked out over the snow and gray trees. "Everybody knows what time it is but me," she sighed.

By the time Emma finished kneading the bread, the baby was crying hard. Ellie's ball of dough looked like it had been made with ashes instead of flour, but Emma put both aside to rise. When it was baked, she'd suggest that Ellie let the chickens have her bread.

She changed the baby and sat down to nurse him. Did she imagine it, or was it easier to sit today?

So far the boys hadn't said a word about Papa coming home today, and Emma wasn't about to raise their hopes by mentioning it. At times the snow in the air was so heavy she couldn't see the woods. She shivered, thinking of Al walking thirteen miles in the blinding storm. She could almost hear Ma talking with Pa. "Think Al will make it home today? He always stops." And Pa would just grunt.

Ma always had a little bag waiting for Al to take to the children and bits of family news to send along. Sometimes there was even a letter from Gustie. A pang of loneliness for her big sister swept over Emma. Gustie, the daredevil. Gustie, the strong, laughing one. Was she still laughing after losing three little girls with croup? Were little Luke and John all right? Had the new baby come? Suddenly Emma wanted to know so badly she groaned. "Oh, Lord. Please let me hear from her." Then she shook her head. "I don't see what good it does to pray, but I guess I'll keep on."

When the baby was content again, Emma went to wash dishes. No water. She'd take two pails to give her balance, she decided. At noon, when she watered the stock, she'd carry more. But when was noon? If only the sun would shine.

Coming back with the water pails, she couldn't even see the house at times through the blowing snow. How could Al possibly get home?

While the water heated for dishes, Emma stretched out on the bed to rest while she could. It wouldn't be easy to get down to the river to water the stock. She had hardly begun to relax when Fred dropped a stick of wood on his toe and cried. Then Albert called him a baby, so Fred hit him and Albert hit him back, and Ellie got in the way and fell into the house of sticks they were building and knocked it down, and Albert cried because she wrecked it. . . .

Emma got up to make peace. *There's no sense washing dishes now*, she decided. *It seems like a long while since breakfast; I may as well feed the children again.* She helped them get started putting the wood in the wood box, and while they were busy, she scrambled eggs.

While they were eating, Emma put the bread in tins and patted some dough in a shallow pan for *Kaffee Kuchen*. She made indentations with her fingertips, poured melted butter over it, and sprinkled it with cin-

namon and sugar. It would be nice to have ready when
Al got home before supper. *If* Al got home.

Later, Emma left the dishes standing and rocked Ellie.
Albert came and whispered in her ear, "Can I have some
paper when you go out?"

She winked and nodded. When Fred wasn't looking,
she whispered in Albert's ear, "Why don't you cuddle in
with Fred and sing him to sleep?"

Ellie's eyelids fluttered, then they were still. "Such a
little dolly," Emma said to herself as she looked down at
the delicate pink cheeks and dark curls. "And I hardly
take time to look at her."

By the time Emma was ready to go out, Albert was
wiggling impatiently at the table. Quietly she took down
more paper and sharpened the pencil. "I hope they
sleep till I get back, but if they don't—"

"I know, Mama. Don't let 'em climb."

She smiled and gently closed the door behind her. *I'd
have to be awfully thirsty to go out in this storm,* she
thought as she opened the barn door. The ox hesitated a
moment but then moved out, and the cows plodded
along behind him.

Although her knees were scabbed now, they still hurt
dreadfully when she knelt down by the water hole, and
spears of pain shot up her back. As she hauled bucket after bucket, she choked back the urge to pray for strength.
"God could have sent someone to help me," she muttered under her breath. If He didn't choose to help her,
she reasoned, she'd just have to do it on her own.

When the animals were back in the barn, Emma
leaned against the log wall for a moment before cleaning
the gutters. She had never let the barn get this dirty before. She picked up the shovel, which seemed to be
made of solid iron, and then set it back down. Al could
do the cleaning with such little effort. It would have to
wait until he got around to it. She latched the door and
struggled through the snow, gasping when the wind

swept her breath away.

"When I'm in the house, warm and dry," she told herself, "I'll just have to face it: Al isn't going to be able to get home." In the lean-to, she stomped her feet and tried to brush off the clinging snow.

"Give it to me, Fred!" she heard Albert yell as she opened the door. Her eyes, accustomed to the blinding glare, refused to see in the dim room. She strained to make out their figures on a chair under the corner shelf. What were they fighting over? Oh, no! Al's straight edge razor! Fred held it, open, in his hand, and Albert hung on to it by the handle, trying to pull it away from him.

"Albert! Let go! Drop it, Fred!"

For one eternity-long instant no one moved, then the razor clattered to the pine floor. Fred wailed, "I jus' wanted to s'ave—like Papa!" Albert streaked away, leaving Fred to her mercy.

Unaware of any pain, Emma propped her foot on the chair rung and turned Fred over her knee. "Don't you *ever* take Papa's razor again!" she railed, emphasizing each word with a well-aimed swat. She released him, and he ran howling to the bedroom.

"What next?" she moaned. She saw Albert cowering behind the coats along the wall, wide-eyed and chalky white. "Come here, Albert," she said shakily.

He crept toward her, chin trembling, and she grasped him firmly by the shoulders. "Albert! Fred could have been cut so bad. You know that, don't you? You *have* to watch him better!"

"Oh, Mama! I'll watch better! I'll watch better!" he sobbed.

"It's a good thing you minded me. If you hadn't let go . . ." Her shudder ended with a sob. "Now, go get in bed and don't even *wiggle!*" she ordered, shaking her finger in his face.

She picked up the razor, keen enough to sever bone,

folded it, and put it in her apron pocket. She would hide it well. Clenching her jaws to keep her teeth from chattering, she took off her overshoes and coat. The dirty dishes sat on the table accusing her, but she ignored them. She filled the stove with wood, shoved the bread and *Kaffee Kuchen* in the oven, and threw herself face down on the bed, thinking that if one of the children so much as moved, he'd wish he hadn't.

"I'm done," she wept. "I can't struggle anymore." Her back was cold, but she didn't want to move to reach for a cover. *Let the wind howl and the windows rattle,* she thought. *I don't care. Probably Al will come home next week, or who knows when, and find us all frozen stiff. It'll serve him right.*

From habit Emma started to pray, "Oh, Lord, help me," but she choked back the words. What was the use? God didn't care. Al didn't care. Nobody cared. *Funny,* she thought, *I don't even feel like crying anymore. I just want to die.*

Thump! Bump! There was someone at the door!

Emma scrambled to her feet, smoothed her hair, and pulled her apron straight on the way to open it. She was halfway across the room when it burst open and a man, so snow-covered she couldn't tell who it was, stood in the doorway.

"Help me with these confounded buttons!" Al's voice boomed as he pulled his snow-crusted "turkey" off his back and dropped it with a thump.

The children flew out of the bedroom. "Papa! Papa!"

"Wait now! Let Papa shake off his coat," Emma yelled over the din. She dug the snow out from around his buttons, then she held back the children so Al could shake his coat out the doorway.

She hurried to the bedroom to lay out dry clothes for him, calling, "How on earth did you get home in this storm?"

"Got a ride with Aaron Nelson to his house!" he

yelled back. "Only had to walk the last couple miles."

"Oh, dear," Emma said to herself. "He didn't get to stop at Ma and Pa's. Ma must be so disappointed."

Albert bounced on his toe. "You got to ride on his sleigh, with the horse?"

"Yup! Sure did. I'll tell you all about it soon as I get dry clothes on."

Albert kept up a steady stream of chatter as Al changed, while Fred and Ellie bounced and squealed. Why was Mr. Nelson the first one to have a horse, Albert wanted to know. Was he rich? Where did he get it? How much did it cost? What color was it? What did the sleigh look like?

Al explained that Mr. Nelson wasn't what some people consider "rich," but he thought a horse was important, and that he shared it with other people whenever he could.

The boys scampered along beside him as he carried his wet clothes to the door and hung them on hooks. Ellie waited, her arms in the air, while he buttoned his vest. When he finished he swooped her up, hugged her, and tossed her in the air. She squealed and laughed, while the boys yelled, "My turn! My turn!"

Al grinned over his shoulder at Emma and called over the children's clamor, "Bread smells good. Almost done?"

"Bread's not, but the *Kuchen* is," she said. "Coffee'll be ready in a minute."

She'd wait, Emma decided, to tell him about her struggles until the first excitement of being home died down. Besides, she needed to sort out her feelings, too. She wasn't sure she wanted to let go of that put-out feeling toward Al. He hadn't asked her how she was, or how things had gone—just came in and started making demands right away. Still, it was so good to hear his voice, to hear the little ones laugh, to have his huge frame almost fill the room.

"Well, hello, little fella," she heard Al say in the special tone he reserved for babies. He picked Georgie up and held him at arm's length, and the baby wiggled and laughed. "Look at 'im laugh, will ya?"

He sat down in the rocker with the baby in one arm, Ellie in the other, and one boy hanging on each knee. "Well, now . . . you guys got anything to tell me?"

"Ellie tore the catalog," both boys tattled in unison.

Al frowned. "Hey. You wouldn't want anyone telling on you, would ya?"

Emma turned the hot *Kuchen* out on a clean dish towel before she explained, matter-of-factly, what had happened. *Just let him yell because I gave them the catalog,* she thought. *He'll get it with both barrels. I'd like to know what he'd have done in my place.*

She was almost disappointed when he ignored the incident and came to the table, a little one still in each arm, dragging a boy on each leg. He told them how fast the horse pulled the home-made sleigh, while Emma poured coffee, cut the *Kuchen*, and took the baby. Ellie clung to Al, daring Emma to make her move.

Albert took a drink of milk, leaving a white mustache. "Can we get a horse and a sleigh? Can we?

Al grinned and nodded. "Yup! Pretty soon. Pretty soon."

He talked on about the week's work, but Emma hardly heard him. His words were drowned out by the screaming in her mind, *What about me? What about what went on here while you were gone?*

Several times she tried to break into his monologue but, failing, retreated into silence. *If he'd just look at me,* she thought, *he could see I've had trouble.*

"Your Ma sure bakes good," Al said to the boys, his mouth so full his words were mushy.

Sure, that's all you care about—your wants, she screamed silently.

He held up his cup. Emma struggled to her feet, babe

in her left arm, and got the coffeepot from the stove.

Al glanced up at the clock. "What on earth? The clock's stopped!"

She nodded. "I forgot to wind it last night."

"You forgot to wind it?" he boomed. You'd think she had said she'd forgotten to feed the baby.

Now was her opening. She wouldn't tell him how bad it had really been. He might think she was making it worse, and he hated exaggeration.

"I—I had a little accident. Cora kicked me."

"What? You let old Cora kick you?" Al slapped his knee and roared with laughter, and the children started to laugh, too. "Emma! I'm surprised at you. You know that old crosspatch! How come you let her get you? And what's that got to do with the clock not being wound, anyway?"

Emma gulped. "Well, it happened Thursday night. I was just putting the stool down; I hadn't even touched her—"

Al pushed back his chair and set Ellie down. "You can tell me about it at suppertime. Looks like the snow is stopping now, so I'd better get some shoveling done while it's still light. Wanna help me, boys?"

They ran to pull on overshoes and coats.

Emma held the tears back until the three were out the door. She could hardly see to take the bread out of the oven and put the roast in. "He could have at least set the clock before he went out," she sobbed.

What a joke her daydreams had been—Al putting her to bed, urging her to rest. He hadn't even come near her.

When she thought about him not stopping at Ma and Pa's, she cried some more. "And he didn't even ask if I got hurt," she sobbed, tears dripping into the dishwater. "And he *laughed*."

She thought of crawling back to bed, leaving the dirty dishes, the wet baby, the soggy clothes by the door, the potatoes unpeeled, and Ellie wailing by the window. But she kept plodding along, doing what needed to be done, crying all the while. About the time she thought she was cried out, she'd remember Al's laughter and start all over again.

What seemed like a long while later, Albert poked his head in the door. "Papa wants to know if supper's ready, or should he do chores first?"

"Tell him to do chores first. Wait! Take some water to the chickens." She fixed warm, not hot, water for him to carry. "I need water in here too," she said, giving him the empty pail as well.

While she peeled the potatoes and limp carrots, Emma planned how she would tell Al he'd have to stay home. She'd wait until the children were in bed. "One more week," she'd say.

There was so much she should do—carry out the ashes, shake rugs, sweep the floor. She stared out the window at the pale light from the barn window, feeling more lonesome than ever. The ashes and the floor could wait, she decided, and sat down with her knitting. Ellie, having given up her window watch, played contentedly with blocks beside her.

I'll tell him it just isn't safe for the little ones. My heart's in my throat the whole time I'm outside, and I can't take them all with me. What would have happened if I had been hurt worse and couldn't walk at all?

She thought of other Saturday nights and how she'd bustle around cooking a good supper and tidying up the house while Al did chores. As she worked, she'd hum tunes that Al would play later on his accordion. She'd listen so hard that through the week she could hear it again. But tonight even the anticipation of the music didn't thrill her.

We've got to get this settled. It won't be easy. I have to say, "Al, I've got something important to talk about." He'll have to listen instead of talk, for once.

Once they got that settled, and he'd promised to quit next week, they could talk about other things. It would be good to hear what was going on in the world. Sometimes Al even brought a newspaper home, but not tonight. Not even a note from Ma.

It must be time to set the table, she thought. She let Ellie put on the forks and a knife for Al and for her. Then she made a fresh pot of coffee and added a little water to the roast. The potatoes and carrots tucked around it were almost done. It smelled so good Emma could hardly wait for supper.

"*Liebchen, Liebchen,*" she crooned as she sat down in the rocker with Ellie. " I know how you feel. It doesn't seem like Papa is ever going to get done with chores."

She sang to Ellie, song after song, but her mind wasn't on the words. She was thinking that she felt more lonesome now that Al was home than before. There was so much to say and no chance to say it.

Al doesn't know what it's like cooped up here like a setting hen day after day. He doesn't know what it's like to work like crazy, so I can get back in here with the little ones. He's working out there now with his mind free; he doesn't have to give a thought to what's going on here.

I don't care if we don't have money; I can't take any more of this trying to do a man's work along with a woman's.

"Mama! Sing!" Ellie demanded.

"Bring them in! Bring them in! Bring them in from the fields of sin," Emma sang. "Bring the wandering ones to Jesus."

She sang on, while in her mind having a conversation with Jesus, telling Him if that He'd take care of this situation, she might have faith in Him again. *But I can't see that you've done very much lately,* she told Him. Then her face flushed. *I have to admit Al got home when I didn't think he would. I suppose that could have been Your doing. I want to trust You, Lord. I need to trust You. I don't know what I'm going to do all those days after Sunday.*

Sunday was tomorrow! She saw herself bundling up Al's clothes into his turkey. He'd swing it up on his back, and off he'd trudge again. Her stomach knotted. *One more week in camp. That's all!*

The baby began to cry. Emma let Ellie hold the pins while she changed him, telling her what a big, helpful girl she was.

"Watch for Papa and the boys," she urged Ellie, as she sat down to nurse George. She had barely gotten settled before she heard their voices, and Ellie was running to the door. "Papa! Papa!"

They'll just have to wait a few minutes for supper, Emma decided. She wasn't about to put the baby down before he was content. With a mixture of pleasure and envy, she listened to their laughter as they stomped in. Al set the milk on the table and went back out for water. The boys scuffled and hollered and made Ellie cry, but they calmed down when Al came in.

"Wash your hands," he ordered as he poured water into the washbasin for them and rolled up his sleeves. He turned to Emma. "That barn sure was a mess. Looked like you didn't clean it all week."

She opened her mouth to explain, but shut it again. This was certainly no time to discuss the matter, and she wasn't going to try to out-yell the children. Besides, she knew she couldn't explain without crying.

The boys scrambled up on the bench behind the table and began drumming with their spoons until Al yelled, "Hey! Enough of that!" They stopped drumming, but kept pushing and shoving each other.

Al ignored them, took his watch out of his vest pocket, and set the clock hands at half past six. "Still can't figure out how you could forget to wind the clock, Emma," he called to her.

"Eat! Eat!" Ellie yelled, banging her plate.

Al frowned at her, and she stopped her banging.

He looked questioningly at Emma. "Want me to dish up?"

"You can take the roast out. I have to thicken the gravy." Stiff-lipped, Emma finished the supper and set it on the table. She dished up food for the children and cut their meat. Then she filled her own plate and was about to take a bite when Al held out his empty coffee cup.

"He could pour his own coffee once," she grumbled to herself as she got up to get the coffeepot. Pain shot up her spine.

Al was so engrossed in telling the boys about what they ate in camp he didn't even notice her grim expression.

". . . and we always have pie for dessert—sometimes cake, too."

Fred listened, round-eyed. "We gonna have pie, Mama?"

"No, we're not having pie. You can have some jelly on your *Kuchen.*"

"Ah, Mama, we *never* have pie," Albert complained.

The roast that had smelled so delicious stuck in Emma's throat. She felt like throwing down her fork and running, but where, she didn't know. *Never enough. No matter how hard I work and how hard I struggle, there's always more I should have done. I didn't have supper on the table when they were ready to eat. Didn't clean the barn. Didn't have pie for dessert.* One more, and she'd tumble in a heap like Ellie's blocks.

She managed to eat a little and to answer Al when he talked to her, but she was glad when supper was over.

Seven

A Vision of Horses

Emma was swishing the bar of soap in the dish-water when she heard Al's yell. "Where in thunder is my razor?"

Hastily she dried her hands and scurried to the bedroom. When she handed it to him, he scowled. "What's it doing in the bedroom?"

She cleared her throat and gripped the back of a chair to keep her hand from trembling. Albert and Fred stopped running and glued their eyes on her.

"I—I came in from watering the stock this noon, and—Fred had it. He was up on a chair by the corner shelf." She took a quick breath. "And he had it —open—in his hand." She shivered. "Albert was trying to pull it away from him."

Emma wanted to go on, to spill out her anguish and say, "See! That's why you have to stay home," but the words wouldn't come. She watched Al put the razor up on the shelf, stoop down and, with smooth motions of his long arms, grasp each boy by a shoulder. He shook Albert, his eyes boring into the small boy's teary ones. "Did your Mama tell you to watch Fred—not to let him climb on anything?"

Albert nodded, his chin trembling.

Then Al shook Fred. "Did your Mama tell you not to climb on anything while she's outside?"

Fred's face crumpled, and he twisted away.

Al shook him again. "Look at me! Did she?"

Fred met his father's eyes briefly, nodded, and began to cry.

Al dropped Albert's shoulder and grasped both of Fred's. The little boy looked up at Al, tears streaming down his face.

Al frowned. "Don't you *ever* climb on anything when your Mama's out doing chores. Understand?"

Fred nodded. As soon as Al released him, he ran like a shot to the bedroom.

Before Albert could run off, too, Al grabbed his arm and said, "You *will* watch the little ones better when Mama is outside."

Albert nodded and disappeared.

Al glanced at Emma. "You spank 'em?"

"I sure did!" She took a step toward Al, so she wouldn't have to talk so loud, but then she stopped. He had turned to the washstand and was whistling as he began mixing his shaving soap.

Tears sprang to her eyes as she went back to her dish washing. *Just like that and it's all over! And he can whistle yet! He can hike out of here, free as a bird. Doesn't he see I can't be two places at once?*

Emma was still prowling around in the dark corners of her thoughts when Al got out his accordion. The little ones went wild before he played the first note.

Oh! It was good to hear music! She washed the oil-cloth on the table absent-mindedly, watching the children's shadows leap high on the walls. She poured the dish water into the slop pail and hung up the dish pan. Then she dried her hands and picked up little Georgie. He sat, wide-eyed, on her lap, and she settled back to enjoy the melody.

If only there were some way to keep the music, so she

could hear it again anytime she wanted to. Emma closed her eyes and let the music wash over her, relieving her, at least for a time, from the load she carried.

Al played one German tune after another while the children danced and pranced and squealed at their grotesque shadows. When he finally closed the accordion with a flourish, the boys pleaded, "One more! Please, Papa! One more."

He began to fasten the strap, but when Ellie toddled over with one pink finger in the air, mimicking the boys, he relented. When they begged again, he said sternly, "To bed now! Lots to do tomorrow."

"Aw . . ." they groaned, but they began to pull off their socks.

Emma sighed. "If only they'd mind me like that," she said to herself. "Most of the time it's as though they don't even hear me."

When the children were in bed, Al pulled a chair close to the stove, propped his wool-stockinged feet up on the edge of the wood box and tilted the chair back. He clasped his hands across his chest and grinned at Emma.

Emma picked up her knitting and tried to sort out just the right words. Now was her chance.

But before she could utter a word, Al was saying, "Oh, Emma, Emma! If only you could have been with me on that sleigh this afternoon. The snow didn't bother that team one bit—they plowed right through. 'Course that little sleigh with a few supplies and the two of us wasn't anything, compared to a load of logs."

He pulled his feet down, and the chair rocked forward with a thud. With his elbow on his knee and chin in hand, he talked on, more to himself than to Emma. "A man could really get ahead with a team. Wouldn't need dynamite for most of the stumps back of the barn. They're rotted pretty good now. A team like that could pull them out like baby teeth." He nodded, staring past Emma. "One more winter in camp, I figure."

He put his feet up on the wood box again and clasped his hands behind his head. Emma sensed a story coming on. Usually she welcomed Al's stories; he could make her feel like she was right there when it happened. But tonight, with words piled up inside her ready to tumble out, she hoped he'd tell it fast.

He cleared his throat and said, "I figure it's about time the Germans got to know the Swedes and the Norwegians better. It's time we found out why they do things the way they do."

"Not me," Emma replied. "If they leave me alone, I'll leave them alone. 'Live and let live,' like Ma used to say. There's room enough for all of us to live the way we're used to living."

"Now, Emma, we're all Americans now. We gotta live together."

"Were you going to tell me something that happened at camp?" she asked, eager to get the story told.

"Oh, yeah. There's this old Swede. His name is John, but everyone calls him Old Peterson."

"I know. You've talked about him before."

"Well, one night Old Peterson told me how three of the families happened to come and settle here. They came over from Sweden about twenty years ago to live in Albany, New York. Then a real estate man talked them into going to work on farms near Sheboygan, Wisconsin.

"Well, life wasn't much better there than it had been in Sweden, so they kept looking for something better. One day they heard about the new railroad that would run all the way from Menasha—that's on Lake Winnebago—"

"For goodness sakes, Al, I know that," Emma said impatiently. "I was born in Oshkosh, you know."

If Al was aware of her impatience, he ignored it. "Well, they heard it would go all the way to Ashland on Lake Superior. They knew that there would be homestead land opening up all along the rail line and figured they'd scout around and see if they could find good land. But they couldn't get away from the farm work until August when the hay was in and before the oats were ripe enough to harvest.

"They took the train to Wausau—just John and his friends, Gust and Ole, not their whole families. In Wausau they found there was a tote road to some lumber camps north of Jenny. It went right through the place where some German families were already homesteading along the Spirit River. They hiked to Jenny and stayed overnight there. They went to the store to buy some grub, enough for a couple of days, and met another Swede in the store."

Al got up to put wood in the stove, and Emma knitted furiously, waiting for him to get on with the story.

"Well, that fella told 'em they'd be foolish to buy food, when they could eat at the lumber camps free, so they just bought a loaf of bread and a ring of bologna to eat till they got to the first camp. He—the other Swede—said he had worked for a man by the name of Isaac Stone. He told 'em about hay meadows about half a mile from Stone's camp. Good homestead land, they figured."

"So did they find the meadows?" Emma asked, hoping to move the story along a bit faster.

"Hold on! Things didn't go quite that easy. This other Swede told 'em to head north of town up along the Wisconsin River to Grandfather Falls and to cross there and keep going on that tote road to McCrossin's camp. He said there was an Irish cook there that never turned anyone away without a good meal, and at Stone's camp there was a cook, Mrs. Johnson, who baked the best pies a man ever ate. Their mouths were about watering already.

"He told 'em they could sleep at the camps, too, on hay in the barn, and that was all right with them. They figured they'd sleep at McCrossin's camp and then go on to the Spirit River the next day."

Emma tried to listen to Al's story, but her thoughts kept slipping back to what she wanted to tell *him*.

"They started north from Jenny, feelin' good about not having to buy food and being able to save some money. They found the tote road and didn't have any trouble crossing at the falls. They ate their bread and bologna and sure were hungry when they saw McCrossin's camp up ahead. A good supper and a night's sleep, and they'd go on to the meadows the next day. But before they got real close to the camp, they figured something was wrong. It was just too quiet."

Emma's knitting lay idle in her lap now. "There wasn't anyone there!"

"That's right! Not a soul. It was deserted."

"Oh, my! Those poor, hungry men!"

"Well, Old Peterson said, they found some hay to sleep on and wished they could tell that Swede a thing or two. The next morning they started out with their stomaches growling. They saw some German log houses along the way. Each time they saw one, Ole wanted to stop and ask for something to eat, but the other two said they'd starve before they'd ask a German for food. They laughed at the way the log houses were built and said the Germans didn't know how to use a broadax or an adz. They said, 'Only tool a German knows how to use is a grub hoe'."

Al chuckled. "Can't blame 'em. You know, a lot of Swedes used to be shipbuilders, and they—"

"So," Emma interrupted, "did they get anything to eat at Stone's camp?"

Al shook his head. "Nope! That camp was deserted, too. That Swede they talked to didn't know that the camps shut down for the summer."

"Well . . . what did they *do?*"

"They saw a porky, and Gust wanted to shoot it. He

had a sawed-off Harper's Ferry loaded with shot, but the others said they wouldn't eat porky, no matter what. By the time they got through arguing, the porky was gone. Finally, they got to the meadows. Gust told the other two to go look at the meadows while he caught some fish. He made a hook out of a piece of wire and was sure he'd catch some."

Again Al let his chair down with a thump and leaned forward. "Those meadows were *good*—bigger than the men had dreamed they would be, and they decided it sure would be the right place to homestead. But Gust hadn't caught any fish. They crawled into Stone's camp hungry as a bear in spring and slept on the cook shanty floor." Al laughed. "I bet they had a few choice things to say about that Swede.

"The next morning they didn't even feel like moving, and here they had all that way to hike to Jenny. Before they left, Gust started hunting around and saw something way down in the bottom of a barrel. He reached down and grabbed a handful and took it over to a window to see what it was. What do you think, Emma? Dried fruit! I don't know just what—apples, prunes and such, I suppose. There were some specks of mold on it, but they didn't care. There musta been a couple pounds, Old Peterson said."

Emma laughed. "I can just see those starved men trying to chew that hard, dry stuff."

Al chuckled. "Bet they didn't have their mouths empty all the way back to Jenny! But at least the trip wasn't for nothing. The next year they filed claims at Wausau and brought their families up and settled. I pass pretty close to Gust's house on the way to Ogema. They did get work at Stone's camp and got to eat Mrs. Johnson's pies all right—but nothing ever tasted better than that moldy dried fruit from the old barrel!"

Emma smiled. For the last ten minutes or so, it was as if someone else had carried her load of trouble.

Al got up and took a drink of water from the dipper in the water pail. "Someday when I've got a little time, I'm gonna stop and take a look at Gust's house. Sure looks solid. The corners look like they're locked in like this." He demonstrated by interlacing his fingers. "Bet a man could move that house and it wouldn't give two inches. Gotta admire their building skill, just like I admire Old Peterson's skill with horses."

Emma shivered. "Fire's burning down," she said flatly.

Al got up and put more wood in the stove. "Yup! One more winter oughta do it," he said, gesturing with the poker.

He stuck his feet up on the wood box again. "I'll cut the pine closest to the river first. Skid it out with the horses and deck it up by the river. By golly, we'll drive it right down that river with the lumber companies' logs!"

"How'll you know which are yours?"

"I'll stamp 'em with a stamp hammer with my own mark on it. And I'll cut a watermark about six inches from the end, so no one can cut my mark off and put his on."

"Oh. But, Al, you said the next thing we would buy would be my sewing machine."

Al nodded. "Gotta get that, too. A few more young ones come along, and you'll never keep up with all that sewing."

Emma wanted to scream, *"What's the use! Sewing machine or no sewing machine, I can't keep up, anyway!* But Al's words had caught her up in his enthusiasm again.

He turned to face her now, the way little Albert did when he wanted to tell her something important—something confidential. "I've been hanging around Old Peterson a lot. I told you how no one knows horses better'n him. He's teaching me a lot. At first I pretended I just wanted to help him, but he was suspicious of anyone wanting to do extra work. So I told him straight out that I wanted to learn about taking care of horses. I think it kinda made him feel good to have someone want to learn from him. If I work with him awhile, I'll learn to be a good teamster, too. Gotta know how to handle horses to get the most out of them."

"Horses! Horses!" Emma muttered to herself. "That's all I hear."

"Ah, can't you see us, Em? Soon as chores are done Sunday mornings, you'll get the little ones ready and I'll hitch up the team. We'll have a buggy for summer and a little cutter for winter, and we'll go see your folks or go to Knox to see Winnie and Jack or out to see Fred and Louise. . . ." He slapped his knee. "Can't you just see Fred, when we pull up in that buggy?"

The thought of seeing her brother Fred brought tears to Emma's eyes. It had been so long. "But that would take all day!" she protested.

"Naw! We could get to Fred's in an hour and to your folks in half that time!"

Emma blinked back tears. Imagine getting to her folks' house in half an hour!

"'Course we'll probably have a church by that time. We'll go to church first, and in summer you could pack us a lunch and we'd stop and eat on the way when the weather is nice."

Al didn't even notice Emma's tears. He was off dreaming again, staring at the rough ceiling boards. "And there's no reason why I can't haul hemlock bark to Rib Lake to the tannery. . . ."

"The what?"

"The tannery. I told you about it last week."

Emma shook her head. "You didn't tell me about it."

"Come to think of it, I didn't hear about it till this week."

A smile tugged at the corners of Emma's mouth as

she watched his eyes shine with little-boy eagerness.

"Fellow named Shaw is building a tannery in Rib Lake. I hear he's gonna need no end of hemlock bark. That's why he's building it here—because of all the hemlock. They use it to tan the hides. Call it 'tan bark.' I don't know exactly how it's done. It's supposed to be starting up this summer." Al leaned forward. "You know, we got almost as much hemlock as pine on our land. Always wondered what on earth I'd do with it." He pounded his fist into his palm. "And here comes that tannery, less than fifteen miles away."

He got up and paced between the door and the stove. "Best part is that the bark'll peel after the snow's gone for hauling logs. A man can peel clear up to the fourth of July, they say. 'Course it will take awhile to get the money for it, 'cause I'll have to wait till it snows again to haul it outta the woods and into town. But I've been thinking, there's no reason why I can't peel some this spring, so it's ready to haul when we get the team."

"I suppose. But we haven't got that team yet, you know."

"Aw, we'll have it. Have to go ahead and dream, or a person never does anything. Dreams always have to come first."

"I've been doing a little dreaming, too," Emma ventured, her eyes on her knitting. "I thought sometime we might sell butter and eggs and things in Tomahawk. You know—to the boarding houses."

Al rubbed his chin thoughtfully. "Hmm . . . good idea. It would take the better part of the day, now; it's twenty miles. But when we get the team, we can do it." He grinned. "You could shop at Oelhafen's and pick out dress goods for you and Ellie."

"That would be nice," Emma said wistfully. "But I'd be satisfied just to go see Ma and Pa."

"By golly! I clean forgot!" Al jumped up and dug a little packet out of his coat pocket. "Your Ma sent this along when I stopped."

"You stopped?"

"Sure! Aaron said he'd wait. I just stood by the door a minute, 'cause I was fulla snow."

Carefully Emma pulled off the store string and opened the packet.

"A letter from Gustie!" she squealed. Quickly she examined the other items: a piece of red ribbon, enough for a bow for Ellie's hair; a little brown bag holding a few round white peppermint candies; some pictures cut from a magazine of a train, a lady talking on a telephone, and a man and lady all dressed up, sitting in a two-seated surrey drawn by a team of dark horses. She handed that one to Albert.

He laughed. "Think we'll ever dress up like that? I can't quite see you wearing ostrich plumes."

Emma wasn't listening. She was reading Gustie's letter, lips moving as she read. "Oh, I'm so glad! The baby was born in January. Doesn't say anything about expecting again. She probably is, though."

When she finished she slipped the letter back into the envelope and held it between her hands. "Gustie says she'll come down on the train sometime next summer, if we can meet her at Ogema."

Al poured hot water in the washbasin and began to scrub his body.

"When you write, you tell her we're gonna get a team and then we can meet her at Ogema," Al said confidently.

Emma sat with her eyes closed seeing horses . . . horses. She could see her mother and father waiting in the doorway as she and Al drove up with the four little ones snuggled in the cutter. She could see Gustie getting off the train with her four little boys and Fred, her brother, giving her a big bear hug when they went to visit him. And Winnie! Winnie would cry; her tears came easily.

She could see Al skidding logs, the horses' muscles

rippling as they moved along at twice the speed of the ox. Al could earn twice as much in camp with a team. A thrill ran through her. Why, if they had a team it would be like Al was working two winters at the same time!

In her imagination she saw him hook a chain on a stump, saw the horses strain, harness taut, saw the stump slowly release its grip from the soil. She saw smooth fields after the stumps had been pulled out and Al had plowed them—crops growing in straight rows, not in spots here and there between the stumps. She saw the horses prancing along the road toward Toma-hawk, Al riding in the light, new buggy loaded with butter and eggs and vegetables to sell.

Al *had* to stay in camp. Somehow, Emma had to manage alone. If only she could count on God to take care of the children while she was outside. But He hadn't sent help when she needed it so badly. It must be that He had more important things to do than take care of little children in log cabins.

Emma took a deep, determined breath as she took out her hair pins and braided her hair for the night. *I'll just have to do the very best I can.*

"Time for bed," Al announced, playfully slapping Emma on the knees as he walked by.

She gave a little cry of pain, making him stop short. "What's the matter?"

Shyly, she pulled up her skirt, pulled down her stock-ings and unwound the sticky bandages, wincing as she pulled them loose from the sores.

"What in thunder . . .?"

"I told you Cora kicked me. . . ." Emma fought pent-up tears. "I fell and struck my spine on the edge of the gutter."

Al frowned. "What's that got to do with your knees?"

"I couldn't walk back to the house—my legs kept go-ing out from under me. I had to keep setting the milk pail ahead of me and crawl, and the ice cut my knees."

She had to get away before she cried like a baby. Al hated crybabies. "I have to get a bandage," she croaked and stood up.

Al stepped in front of her and drew her gently into his arms. "How's your back now?"

"Better."

"When did this happen, Emma?"

"Thursday night." Al's arms felt so strong, so safe. There was no holding back the sobs now. "My back hurt so bad. I had an awful time watering the stock . . . and I lost my milk, and the baby cried and cried. . . ."

He held her close, swaying gently. "Go ahead. Cry it out," he said softly.

When she had quieted, he said, "You get to bed now. I'm gonna sit up a few minutes and fill the stove again."

It was several minutes before Emma stopped trembling. She lay rigid, waiting for Al to come to bed. She heard him fix the fire. The house went black as he blew out the lamp. Then the bed creaked under his weight.

Emma tensed.

Gently Al tucked the covers up around her neck and turned on his side—away from her.

Slowly Emma let her breath out and smiled in the darkness. Ma was right: Al was no ordinary man. Her body relaxed, but her mind was still at work. He hadn't said a word to let her know that he was concerned.

Sometimes, she told herself, *it doesn't pay to act strong. A man thinks you can handle anything.* Would he go back to camp without talking things over with her, without letting her tell him her fears, without making some arrangements for someone to stop by more often? Did he really care?

Father, she began to pray, *I'm in a spot. I want to trust You, but I don't know what to think. So far You haven't helped me much. I see now that Al's just gotta stay in camp. We need those horses.*

But how am I going to keep these little ones safe? What if I get hurt again, or one of them gets sick? How will I keep going for all those weeks until the snow is gone . . . and then through another whole winter? And what if I have another baby by then?

Eight

Bittersweet Beauty

Emma woke with a start. *The fire! What time is it?*

Relief flooded over her when she heard Al shaking down the ashes. Ahh . . . she could stay in bed. She could stay in the house. She wouldn't have to go out until milking time tonight.

She stretched and winced. It wouldn't be a pain-free day.

Emma couldn't remember when she had slept so soundly and for such a long time. It must have been the security of having Al by her side that allowed her this blessed sleep. She hadn't even heard him get up to put wood in the stove during the night. And the baby had slept, too. He must be getting enough to eat again. As though he had overheard her thoughts, Georgie whimpered and was quiet again.

When she heard Al go out to do chores, Emma burrowed a little deeper into the warm covers. Her thoughts turned to what she had to do today. "Oh my goodness!" she groaned. "I completely forgot to wash Al's socks and underwear last night."

She rolled out of bed and pulled the little tub of

water Al had filled the night before over the hot stove
lids. Someday they'd buy a stove with a reservoir, and
she wouldn't have to see that old tub on the stove all
the time.

She decided to dress while the children were still
sleeping, but she had hardly buttoned her dress and put
the pins in her pug when the baby announced that he
wanted to eat—now.

Settled in the rocker with the baby at her breast,
Emma thought about the team of horses again. Last
night she had been so excited about all they would do
when they got the horses, she had felt equal to any challenge—even being alone with the children for another
winter. But now, in the early morning gray, a knot of
fear clutched her middle at the thought of Al trudging
off to camp again.

"I've got to talk to him," she told herself. "I've got to
tell him how bad it was. There must be *something* we
can do. Right after breakfast, we'll talk." She thought
again of her daydream about Al coming home, putting
her tenderly to bed, and saying he didn't know how she
had managed to get through all those hours.

Emma sighed. "That sure was a dream! I can do
without praise, but at least he could tell me he knows I
had a rough time. I wish I could talk to Kate or Ma or
someone!"

Objects in the room were taking shape by the time the
baby had finished nursing, but Emma still needed to
light the lamp to see to wash Al's things. She opened
Al's turkey and took out the soggy socks and underwear.
*I'll have to finish knitting his new socks before next
weekend*, she thought, as she examined a pair almost beyond darning. She scrubbed and rinsed and wrung,
scolding herself for not washing them last night. She
wrung each one until she couldn't extract another drop,
then hung them on the rack behind the stove and reminded herself to turn them often so they would be dry

by the time Al had to leave. If only he had enough socks and underwear that he could take clean ones and leave these home for her to wash during the week. But underwear and yarn cost money.

"Money! Money!" she muttered. "No matter where I turn, we need money." She stirred oatmeal into boiling water and was almost done setting the table when the boys woke up. Of course they woke Ellie, who began to cry until she remembered Papa was home. Out she flew, bare feet pattering across the cold floor calling, "Papa? Papa?"

"Papa's still in the barn. Come. Let's get dressed before he comes in."

"Boys!" she called as she dressed Ellie. "I've got a surprise for you as soon as you're dressed."

"What? What?" they clamored.

"I can't tell you till you're all done dressing."

They ran out of the bedroom in moments, still struggling with buttons.

Emma opened the little brown packet and spread the pictures on the table. "See, Fred! That's a train."

"I want the twain," he yelled grabbing it.

Luckily Albert wanted the horses, or there would have been a squabble.

Emma handed Ellie the telephone picture. Soberly the little girl turned it over and back again, looking up at Emma for an explanation.

"Here, *Liebchen*, I'll put it away for you. When you're bigger, I'll tell you all about telephones. You'll like this better." She pulled out the red ribbon. "See! Mama'll make you pretty! Let me tie it in your hair, and you'll look pretty when Papa comes in."

When it was secure Ellie patted it, eyes questioning. Emma picked her up and let her see herself in the wavy walnut-framed mirror. The pain that shot up Emma's spine almost took her breath away, but Ellie's delight was worth the cost, she told herself as she set her down.

A chorus of "Papa, look! Papa, look!" greeted Al when he came in from doing chores. Emma felt a twinge of envy. They never greeted her with such exuberance.

While Emma tied a flour-sack towel around Ellie's neck and poured cream on her oatmeal, Ellie waved and jabbered and fussed.

"Eat your oatmeal now! See? Mama put sugar on it!"

But Ellie just banged her spoon and yelled all the more.

The boys showed Al their pictures, and he tried to tell Albert about the horses' harnesses. Ellie's fussing threatened to drown him out.

Al frowned at her. "Ellie! What are you yellin' about?"

She pointed at the boys' pictures. "Mine! Mine!" she insisted.

"Oh, for goodness' sake," Emma said. "She wants her picture."

When Emma gave it to her, Ellie handed it to Al with a big grin.

"That's a telephone," he told her.

Fred looked puzzled. "What's a tele . . . tele—"

"Telephone," Albert informed him, as though he knew all about it.

"Tell Fred what it is," Al challenged.

"Well. . . it's a . . . Mama told me. . . ." He shrugged. "I forgot."

Al smiled. "A telephone," he explained between mouthfuls of oatmeal, "is, well, it's a . . . guess you'd call it an instrument that you use to talk to people who are far away. See," he pointed and the boys craned their necks to look, "this is the receiver where you listen, and this is the mouthpiece. That's what you talk into."

"Did you ever see one?" Emma asked quietly.

"Sure did! Watched a man talkin' on one in town last year. He let me listen."

"Did it sound like a real person?" Albert asked.

"Yup! Sounded far away, though, and there was some crackling sound, but I could hear every word."

"How far away was he?" Albert said, spoon in the air.

"Clear across town."

Emma shook her head. "That's hard to believe."

Albert wrinkled his forehead. "How does the sound get through?"

"I don't know exactly, but it has something to do with electricity."

"Lectricity? What's that?"

Al rolled his eyes and rubbed his chin. "Now, how do I explain that?" he asked Emma. "Well, you can't see it, but it's a power and it can go through wires. Somehow that power is changed back to the sound of the voice again, when it gets to the telephone receiver."

"Where are the wires?" Albert wanted to know.

"They're strung way up high on tall poles all along the streets or roads." Al spread a thick slice of bread with butter. "We'll have a telephone someday."

Albert's eyes widened. "We will?"

"Sure will," Al continued. "The telephone was invented way back in 1876, and here it is 1892. It's high time we got 'em out here where we need 'em."

Emma stared out the window. "Wouldn't that be something. . . ."

Al chuckled. "One thing, we won't have any trouble getting poles for the wires around these parts!"

"Would I be able to talk to my Ma? That's over three miles."

"Sure you could. You could talk to Kate, too. That's called 'long distance'."

Emma's eyes brightened. "But what'll it cost to buy one?"

"As I understand it, you don't buy it. You pay rent on it. The telephone company owns it."

"How soon do you think. . . ."

Al shrugged. "Oh, I don't know. Five, ten years, maybe."

Emma blinked back tears. Al would be home instead of in camp by then. Now was when she needed it.

Al didn't notice her misty eyes and went on telling the boys there would be all kinds of inventions by the time they grew up.

"What's an invention?" Albert wanted to know.

"Well, now, an invention is something someone makes that hasn't been made before. Sleighs had to be invented, and wagons—even stoves. You'll learn a lot about inventions when you go to school."

Albert took a hasty drink of milk, leaving a white mustache above his mouth. "When kin I go to school?"

"Maybe this fall."

"Will Miss Clark be there?"

"I s'pose so."

"She's purdy."

Al and Emma chuckled. "He's a Verleger all right," Al said to Emma. "Knows a pretty girl when he sees one."

Emma ignored the comment. "Jenny Clark looks a lot like Kate's girls, don't you think?"

"Hmm, same red hair, if that's what you mean. Only saw her once, at that corn husking party at Gebers'."

"Albert took a shine to her, and so did Fred," said Emma. "She told me she's English, but it looks to me like some Irishman got over the border. She seems like a nice young lady, but she sure has an odd way of talkin'."

Al laughed. "That's why the county superintendent of schools sends these English girls out in the country. They hope the Germans and Swedes and Norwegians will learn proper English."

"Your Ma would rather have her speak German. When I told her I thought Miss Clark must be pleasant company for her, she started complaining–"

Al interrupted, "You know better than to pay attention to Ma. She'd complain about the Angel Gabriel, if he boarded with them."

Albert tugged on Al's arm. "What's 'boarded' mean?"

"It means a person who pays a family to live with them," Al explained.

"Miss Clark hasta *pay* to live with Grandma and Grandpa Verleger?"

Al nodded and exchanged a smile with Emma. He knew she was wondering, too, if Albert was thinking that someone would have to pay *him* to live with his Grandma Verleger. Though Emma wouldn't allow the children to speak disrespectfully about their elders, Albert was free to think his own thoughts, and many unpleasant incidents had not endeared Grandma Verleger to him.

Al scraped his chair back from the table. "Gotta get the snow shoveled and the barn cleaned."

He had hardly gone outside when he came in again. "Em . . . come here." He draped her coat around her shoulders and ushered her toward the door.

Immediately Albert and Fred scrambled down from the bench. "No! Not you fellas! Get back to the table and finish your breakfast," Al ordered. "Your Mama'll be right back."

He drew her out into the crisp, gleaming-white morning. "We just have to take a minute to enjoy looking at all this," he said.

Emma pulled her coat close around her and shivered. Al stepped behind her and wrapped his long arms around her, his chin resting on her head.

"I like the spruce and balsam up along the edge of the field," he said softly. "Don't even notice the shape of 'em till they've got snow on 'em, like now."

Emma let her eyes rove from the far edge of the field beyond the barn to the pillow-topped barn roof where the snow hung in graceful scallops along the east side of the building. Her eyes followed the intricate curves the wind had carved in the drift close to her feet. It was pretty, all right. But the beauty wasn't penetrating that hollow spot inside of her. It was like trying to pour water into a jar with the lid on. She pulled her thoughts back and tried to listen to Al.

". . . and man thinks he's so smart," Al was saying. "Like to see 'em make something this perfect."

Emma sighed, "I wish it would stay this white."

"You want snow all year?"

"Oh, no! I can't wait for spring, but it's so pretty and clean. Look at it sparkle now that the sun's getting high!"

Al made a wide sweeping gesture with his right hand. "They're diamonds for you, Em. Probably the only kind I'll ever be able to give you," he said wistfully.

"Only kind I want," she said softly. "What use would I have for real ones?"

A bellow from the barn startled both of them.

Al's arms tightened around Emma in a quick hug, then he trotted off toward the barn, calling over his shoulder, "It's Molly. Forgot to tell you, she's calving. Looks like a big one, judging by the hooves."

Molly bellowed again, and Emma cringed. *Poor thing*, she thought. *She's such a little cow to have a big calf.* She turned to go in the house, amazed that she had forgotten Molly was due to drop her calf at any time. She shook her head and muttered, "What would I have done if the calf had come yesterday?"

With one foot on the door sill, Emma hesitated. Maybe if she really tried to think about the snowscape, she could feel the usual happy feeling such beauty brought her. Yesterday's boisterous wind had blown far away, leaving an eerie stillness behind. Soundlessly a ridge of snow toppled and fell from an elm branch near the river. Soon, Emma knew, these branches would all shed their ermine coats; the sparkling snow blanket would become track-marred and dull. Now was the time to take in its beauty.

But the more she tried to absorb it, the emptier she felt, until the sparkles wavered through her tears. "What's the matter with me?" she groaned.

Molly bellowed again, and a chill raced up Emma's spine. She had never heard a cow carry on like that. Maybe she should help. No, the children would be at the door any second.

Still she lingered, her coat wrapped tightly around her. What if they lost the calf after all that time and effort to get Molly bred? There had been a thousand things to do last spring, when they first came back from Phillips. Right in the middle of that first week, Al had to lead Molly ten miles to Spirit Falls to have her bred. When Emma had fretted because Al had to spend all that time on the road, he had reminded her that he might have had to go clear to Tomahawk, if Mr. Bradley hadn't bought a bull and kept him at Spirit Falls for the convenience of the farmers in the area. She had agreed that Mr. Bradley had certainly done them all a good turn, but just the same, there was ground to be tilled and seeds to plant.

Al had reminded her, too, how fortunate they were to have Molly. If Al's mother had had her way, they would have had only Bessie, the cow they had left with his parents when they moved to Phillips—and Cora, of course. Grandma Verleger had been only too glad to get rid of Cora. She had wanted to keep Molly, but Grandpa said his rheumatism was worse than ever and he couldn't lead her all the way to Spirit Falls. So Molly had become theirs.

Now, from the sound of things, neither Molly nor the calf would make it.

As Emma opened the door she said to herself again, "What if the calf had come yesterday, or waited until tomorrow?" She began to thank God for the perfect timing, and for allowing her to forget the calf was coming and sparing her that worry, but she took a deep breath instead.

"Where's Papa?" Albert yelled when he saw her come in.

Emma blinked in the dim room, hung up her coat, and told him that Papa had gone to the barn. Of course, the boys begged to go to the barn, too, and Ellie clung to Emma's skirt and whined.

"Papa'll be in soon," Emma assured them. "When he comes back, we'll see if you can go out with him."

Albert pouted. "He always lets us go with 'im."

Emma began to clear the table, thinking that soon the calving of a cow would be a common occurrence for the boys. But not this one. She'd have to think of something to keep them occupied.

She went to put wood in the stove and noticed that there were only a few sticks left. "Boys! The wood box is almost empty. Hurry and fill it before Papa comes in, and I'll have a surprise for you."

It worked. Albert carried armloads and dumped them into the wood box, Fred dragged in a few sticks, and Ellie got in the way, as usual. At least they were busy.

Emma flipped over the still-wet socks and long-legged underwear.

Perhaps the boys would play contentedly in the fresh snow while Al drank a cup of coffee. Then she'd sit down, look him right in the eye, and say, "Al, we have to do something about my being alone while you're gone."

What they could do, she didn't know. If only Gebers lived closer, so Clara could run over while Emma was outside.

"Mama! It's full!" Albert announced.

"My goodness, it sure is! We'll have enough wood to

last until tomorrow!" Emma exclaimed. "Sit down at the table, and I'll get your treat."

She went to the pantry and got the peppermint candies her mother had sent and gave them each one piece. "Look what Grandma Kamin sent you!"

She popped one into her own mouth, too.

Albert and Fred giggled, and Ellie drooled.

Emma waited a few minutes until she knew the candy was almost gone. Then, eyes twinkling, she said, "Now I have another surprise for you. Come here and take a drink of water and see what happens."

She held the dipper for each of the children, and as soon as one had a drink there were squeals of, "Cold! Cold!"

Emma glanced at the clock. After ten already. She began to slice the leftover venison to heat for dinner and for sandwiches for Al. He wouldn't get to camp until after supper.

Her thoughts turned to poor Molly struggling to have her calf. Again she stifled the urge to pray.

"Papa's comin'!" Albert yelled and dashed to the door.

Emma poured warm water in the washbasin before Al strode in, his hands outstretched in front of him.

"Got a surprise for you boys," he called over his shoulder as he washed his hands. "Get your overshoes and coats on!"

Fred's eyes opened so wide the white showed all the way around the blue. "Another s'prise?"

Al grinned at Emma and whispered, "She did it! Nice big heifer calf."

"Oh! I'm so glad! What happened? How come she had trouble?"

"It's a pretty big calf, and she needed help. I had to really pull!"

"What would I have done if it had come yesterday, or tomorrow?"

Al shrugged. "Helped her."

"How?"

He dried his hand on the roller towel. "You just take a piece of rope and tie it around the little hooves—you've seen how they always come first, unless something's really wrong—and then tie a stick on, so you can get a good grip. When she pushes, you pull!"

"But I'm not strong like you. . . ."

"Just brace yourself against the gutter edge or a post, and use all your weight." Al started for the door without noticing Emma's pale face. "You fellas ready?"

When Ellie saw the boys getting dressed to go outside, she flung herself at Emma, wailing, "Go out! Go out!"

Al smiled down at her. "Get her dressed," he said.

"But she doesn't have any overshoes."

"She won't need 'em. I'll carry her."

"It wouldn't hurt him to dress her," Emma grumbled to herself. But she had to smile as Ellie waved to her over Al's shoulder, tears still glistening on her pink cheeks.

"Mama? You comin'?" Albert yelled from the lean-to.

"No. The baby'll be waking up soon. I'd better stay here."

She watched them from the window, wondering again why she hadn't been able to feel joy when she looked at all that beauty. She went to pick up George, wondering if there was something terribly wrong with her.

Settled in the rocker with the baby, she thought about the calf again. Al made it sound so easy: "When she pushes, you pull." Emma could see herself slipping and landing in the gutter again. Anger welled up inside of her, and tears threatened. He hadn't even mentioned her struggle since she told him about it. "He hasn't the least idea. . . ." she said out loud. "As soon as he comes back in, we're going to sit down and *talk!*"

But Al didn't come in. The boys brought Ellie in and announced, "Papa says to have dinner ready 'bout half past 'leven."

They were bursting with excitement about the calf. "She's got a white spot on her head, an' Papa says it's a star an' we're gonna call her 'Star,' " Albert informed her.

Fred was trying to wedge in some words, so Emma turned to him and ignored Albert. Fred gulped and said, "Ah . . . ah . . . she's all . . . *soft* , an' Ellie gwabbed her ear. . . ."

Albert interrupted, "An' she wouldn't let go!" He started to giggle, and Fred and Ellie joined in, too.

They giggled and jabbered, and Emma nodded and smiled. But inside she was planning what she would say to Al—*right after dinner*.

Nine

The Right Moment

After telling their mama about the calf, the boys had immediately gone back outside. Ellie cried at the window a while before she settled down to play. Momentarily, peace reigned.

As the minutes ticked by, bringing Al's departure ever closer, Emma's glances at the clock became more frequent. Almost half past eleven. He should be in for dinner any minute now.

The fragrance of freshly ground coffee filled the air. It would be the last she would enjoy until Al was home again. Each time she ground coffee, she visually measured the remaining beans and wondered which would come first—the bottom of the jar, or money to buy more. During the week Emma drank piping hot water and milk.

The table was set, bread sliced, leftover potatoes, carrots, and gravy heated. A moment ago she had been eager to eat but now, when she glanced at the clock again, her stomach churned.

Emma tried to push aside thoughts of tomorrow, but back they came again. Ellie would cry and whine all day because she missed her papa but didn't know how to explain how she felt. The boys would miss him, too, and take their feelings out on each other. There would be fights all day.

But Ellie's whining and the boys' fighting would be nothing compared to having to struggle through the chores alone. Emma's back, though considerably improved, was far from better. Slipping on icy bumps would not be pleasant. And the worst part would be rushing, heart in her throat, to get back to the house. What if she, or one of the children, got hurt again?

Tucked here and there between the dread was disappointment. There would be no time for Al to hold her close and give her that all-put-back-together feeling. No time for tender kisses—or any other kind.

No time. No time. During those golden days of the autumn before their summer wedding, Emma had never imagined life would be like this.

She could almost hear the leaves rustle, remembering how she and Al had walked through the brilliant woods that fall—talking and talking. No one had ever cared what she thought before. No one had ever encouraged her to talk, not even her friend Hattie. Emma had always been a listener.

But Al was different. He wanted to know what she thought. Of course he talked plenty, too. Emma listened, enraptured, as he told of his experiences and his dreams for the future—dreams he had shared with no other person.

Al valued her opinion and said she had good common sense. Anyone could get an education if he made the effort, Al had told her, but not everyone could have common sense. He knew Emma had only gone as far as the third reader in school, because she could only go to school when there wasn't much work to do at home. He hadn't got much farther himself. But once a person learned to read, Al said, he could learn all he wanted to by himself.

One thing concerned her, though. She had always

heard that "true love never runs smooth." Could theirs really be true love? They didn't have the stormy quarrels the other girls confessed to. Oh, they disagreed about things, and sometimes it took a lot of talking—pretty loud talking—to get it straightened out, but Al never left with anything unsettled between them.

Emma saw no sense in playing silly games, either. Winter would come all too soon, and Al would go to camp down near Jenny until spring. She was always aware of their limited time together—especially when he held her close.

Each time he came, Emma hoped he would talk about marriage but, to her keen disappointment, he didn't mention it at all that fall. He left one Sunday evening with fervent kisses and assurances that he's miss her, but that was all.

She avoided Ma's searching eyes the day Al left. If only she could have said, "I'm engaged to Al Verleger." Ma encouraged Emma to work on her hope chest. A girl didn't have to be engaged to work on her hope chest.

Emma was touched by Ma's kindness that winter. Ma could be cross and despondent, but that winter she often sang as she worked and made an effort to brighten Emma's days. One time she dug out an old, old quilt pattern and suggested that Emma might want to piece a quilt that winter. They made a big, braided rug, too.

Of course baby Anne brightened their lives. If it hadn't been for her cheery smile and adorable antics, the winter would have been unbearably long.

"Good practice for you," Ma said when Emma bathed and fed her.

Sometimes Emma pretended that Anne was her baby—*their* baby, hers and Al's.

"Spring thaw's early this year," Pa told Ma one day, and Emma's heart leaped. Al would come back to his father's house and start work on his log cabin on his own land again.

At times doubts plagued her. She didn't have to worry about him finding another girl—not in camp. But maybe he had changed his mind about her. Then she would remember those golden fall days and all the laughter and good-natured banter and serious talk and the kisses that left them reeling, and she *knew* he'd be back and things would be the same.

One sunny day early in April, she was out piling wood when she saw Al hiking up the lane. She wanted to run to meet him, but forced herself to pretend she hadn't seen him. It was better to be sure things hadn't changed first.

Al called to her as soon as he rounded the corner of the house. Emma kept her feet still and merely smiled her welcome. As soon as she looked into his eyes, she knew nothing had changed, and a wave of joy left her weak.

"How are you?" he asked huskily.

She smiled up at him. "Fine! Just fine!"

"It was one long winter for me, I can tell you. Was it long for you?"

Head down, Emma nodded.

Al lifted her chin and saw that her eyes were brimming with tears. His arms closed around her so tight she let out a little gasp. "I was afraid you might have found someone else," he said before he kissed her. He held her more gently then, and she didn't ever want to leave the circle of his arms again. "I've got so much to tell you," he said, releasing her.

"Want to go in the house?" she asked, remembering her manners.

"I'd just as soon stay out here, if you're warm enough." She sat down on a block of wood, and Al rolled another one beside her, close enough to keep an arm around her. There they sat, while he told her story after story about camp life, and she told him bits of local news.

The sun disappeared over the barn roof, and Emma shivered.

"You're cold," Al said. "You better go in."

"Will you stay for supper?"

"Can't tonight, but I'll come back as soon as I can."

He gathered her in his arms again when they stood up. "Oh, I missed you! Em, let's get married this summer. I think I can get the cabin ready by . . . around July first. How would that be?"

She couldn't find her voice, so she simply looked up and nodded.

"I'll talk to your Pa soon. Sunday, maybe."

Al came in long enough to greet Ma, and Emma knew she saw the glow in their eyes. She didn't even scold her for sitting outside and talking so long. She didn't ask any questions, either, and Emma had been grateful. She wanted to tell her so badly, but she wouldn't say a word until Al had talked to Pa. Surely Pa wouldn't have any objections—but she couldn't be sure. She was only seventeen.

She barely drew a peaceful breath until Sunday, when Al and Pa had their talk and came in laughing. Ma was obviously pleased. Emma knew she couldn't wait to tell the neighbor ladies that *her* daughter was going to marry Al Verleger. At least two of them were cherishing hopes for their own daughters.

So long ago all that seemed now. Emma tried to recall that wonderful protected feeling Al had given her then. How she had loved to walk at his side, though she had to remind him over and over to shorten his stride so she could keep up. And he had been proud of her accomplishments and the way she coped with difficult times back then. He didn't carry on about those things, but he had ways of letting her know she had done well. It would mean so much now to know that he realized what she had been through while he was away—to know he was proud of the way she managed to get the work done and take care of the children. It would only take a minute.

Work, work, work. That's all he has on his mind. Doesn't he know that feelings are important?

Anger threatened to crowd out her disappointment, but Emma choked it back and wiped her eyes with her apron. "Oh, Al, hurry up!" she whispered as she stared out at the gleaming whiteness, oblivious of its beauty.

Beyond her eagerness to talk to him lay a more profound reason for wanting him back in the house. As soon as Al and the boys came in, the dark thoughts, always at the edge of her consciousness, would recede—the thoughts about God. Eventually, she would have to face those awful doubts, but not now. If God wasn't going to help her, she had to help herself by having it out with Al.

When she heard them coming, she quickly tried to rehearse what she would say to Al after dinner. Into the kitchen they tramped, red cheeks glowing, noses running, the boys laughing and shoving each other. Emma pulled out a piece of soft rag from her apron pocket. "Blow," she ordered each in turn.

"Star's eatin' already," Albert said, "but her legs are real wobbly."

Emma chuckled. "Your legs were more than wobbly the day you were born! You didn't walk for almost a year. This little calf can walk the very first day."

Albert hung up his coat, which promptly fell off the hook. He ignored it.

Emma pointed to it.

He sighed and hung it up, saying, "Calves are smarter than people, huh?"

Emma tried to hide her smile. "Well, not really. Just in some ways. Nature knew mama cows couldn't carry their babies like people can, so calves have to be able to walk right away."

"Oh," he said, looking puzzled. "What's 'nature'?"

"Ah . . . nature is, nature is . . . God. God made everything."

"Then why don't people just say 'God' instead of saying 'nature'?

Before she could come up with an answer, she heard Al stomping off snow in the lean-to. "Quick! Wash your hands before Papa comes," she said as she poured water for them.

"Calf looks good," Al announced.

"How's Molly?"

"Fine."

Emma heaved a sigh of relief.

"I dragged in enough hay to last you this week," he said rolling up his sleeves.

As she dished up the vegetables, Emma muttered to herself, "I need a lot more than hay dragged in from the stack." Then more loudly she said, "Hurry up, boys. Come and eat." But as soon as Al finished washing his hands, he began swinging the boys on his long arms until they squealed with delight. Ellie clung to his leg, squealing, too.

Emma scooped her up and set her at the table, but Ellie screamed and tore off the dish towel Emma tried to tie around her neck. She wanted a ride on Al's arm.

"Just one ride?" Al said, and lifted her down from her chair.

While Ellie rode, the boys tackled his legs. When he set Ellie down, he made a ferocious face, growled, and grabbed a boy in each arm and pinned them to the floor. Ordinarily Emma thoroughly enjoyed their horse-play but now, one eye on the clock, she yelled, "Come on! Dinner's getting cold!"

She bribed Ellie with a piece of bread and syrup and managed to get her seated, the dish towel securely tied.

"The baby will be crying any minute now," she muttered. How he could sleep through this commotion, she didn't know.

Finally, breathless and flushed, the boys slid behind the table on the bench. Al sat down, looked at her intently, and said, "You know, we didn't ask the blessing last night or this morning."

Emma dropped her eyes and nodded. Did Al suspect she wasn't on speaking terms with God? She tensed. What if he asked her to pray? Relief washed over her when she heard his deep voice.

"Father, forgive us for forgetting to thank You. We do thank You for this food and for all You have given to us. And, most of all, we thank You for sending Jesus. In Jesus' name we pray. Amen."

He picked up his fork and shook it at the boys. "Boys! That was a terrible thing we did, forgetting to pray and to thank God. He *has* to have first place in our lives. We just can't forget Him like that. We better not get so caught up with other things. . . ."

His words drifted past Emma as she poked the meat plate at him. A sermon, yet! Absent-mindedly he took the plate. ". . . and when we forget to thank Him . . ."

Emma's jaws tightened as she cut her meat. She chewed a bite and forced it down. "He could have at least prayed for our safety," she grumbled to herself. Anger brought a sting of tears, and she blinked furiously.

"Hey! I forgot to tell you!" Al boomed. "I had my picture taken last week. The whole camp did."

The boys' eyes widened. "You did?"

Al nodded. "A photographer—that's a man who takes pictures—came out to the camp. The woods boss ordered us to load up a sleigh for the picture, and we all stood around it. You should have seen that load! 'Course we were just showin' off—the horses couldn't have pulled that load, but it looked good. Didn't get much work done that afternoon. "

Emma frowned. Al hadn't even taken a bite, and it was after twelve. Only two hours till he had to leave, and he hadn't watered the stock yet.

"You gonna get a picture to bring home?" Albert asked.

Fred waved his spoon. "Kin I see it?"

"How's it get outta the camera?" Albert asked before Al could answer either question.

"Can't tell you now," Al said, glancing at the clock. "I gotta eat. There's a lot to do yet."

"Thank goodness," Emma said to herself when she saw him shovel in his food. "Are you leaving about two?" she asked.

He nodded. "I could use an extra pair of socks this week," he said with his mouth full of food.

Albert started to protest, but Emma shushed him. "Papa knows he shouldn't talk with his mouth full, but this is an emergency."

"What's a 'mergency?"

"It's when something has to be done *right now.*"

"Like when we gotta pick up our blocks *right now?*"

"Well . . . not exactly. I'll explain it better later. I hear Georgie crying."

Emma took a quick gulp of coffee and went to tend the baby. The sooner she got him changed and quiet, the sooner she could talk with Al. Should she get Fred and Ellie down for naps and let Albert go out to play before she tried to talk with him?

"Such a good little boy," she crooned to George, as she laid him on the bed. He stopped crying and grinned.

She heard the door slam. With deft movements she lifted the baby by the ankles, pulled out the soggy diaper, and whipped a dry triangle under him. She pulled the three corners together, pinned it, and swept him into her arms.

When she returned to the table, Al's place was empty! "Papa go out already?" she said, wondering if the boys would sense her dismay.

Albert nodded. "He said he was going to Grandpa's, and we couldn't come along."

"To Grandpa's!" Emma whirled and headed back to the bedroom, too angry to cry. *Less than two hours left, and he goes to his Pa's.* Even with his long legs, it would take him nearly twenty minutes one way, and he'd talk a while, and the stock hadn't even been watered.

The baby screamed, and she swayed with him in her arms until her legs began to tremble so badly that she staggered to the rocker. Of course, the boys were squabbling and Ellie had climbed down from her chair and was crying ant tugging at the towel around her neck. Emma untied it with one hand.

"Go potty now, like a good girl, and maybe Albert will sing to you when you get into bed."

There was no way this tired little girl could stay awake another hour until Al came back. Maybe she'd wake up before he left. Emma groaned. If Ellie got to say good-bye to him, she'd cry and cry when he hiked away. But if she didn't see him go, she'd wake up, find him gone, and still cry. What was the difference. . .

"Albert! Are you done eating? Come here!"

Eventually he came, with Fred right behind him.

"I need you to help me," Emma whispered. "I want to get Fred and Ellie to bed. They'll settle down if you crawl in with them and sing to them."

Albert frowned and stuck out his lower lip.

When Fred glanced away, Emma winked at Albert— meaning, "I'll have a special reward for you."

Albert nodded and grinned.

For once Fred didn't protest about naptime. He raced into the bedroom, squealing and giggling, and Emma had to remind him to go potty first.

Why on earth did Al have to go to his folks' house for? she wondered. He could have made a quick stop on his way to camp. When she put the baby up on her shoulder, her arms were so weak she had to sit him on her lap.

Al's socks! He wanted another pair. She'd have to darn them. With one hand Emma dropped a comforter on the floor, straightened it with her toe, and laid the baby on it. Maybe he would roll around contentedly. It was a good time for him to be on the floor, while no one would be opening the door to let in cold drafts.

Emma struggled to her feet. She could hear Albert singing, but the other two were quiet. Thank goodness! It was working.

Now, what could she give Albert for a reward? Going outside was nothing unusual. Anyway, she wanted him to go out when Al came back. Paper and pencil? That was nothing new, either. There were only enough peppermints for one apiece after Al left. . . . Suddenly she remembered the wallpaper scraps Ma had sent a couple weeks ago.

That was it! She'd stir up a little flour and water paste, and let Albert paper something. But what? Mentally, she roved the house. Ah. The little wooden box under her bed that held yarn. He could cover the whole thing with paper if he wanted to.

She tiptoed to the bedroom, pulled out the box, dumped the yarn on the bed, winked at Albert, and tiptoed out again, her finger over her lips. Fred and Ellie had their eyes closed, but she feared they weren't yet sleeping soundly.

She'd have to clear the table to give Albert room to paste. All the while she set the dishes in the dishpan (she didn't care if they *ever* got washed), her mind spewed out thoughts: *Doesn't he think about what goes on here after he's gone? Does he just walk away and forget us? Sure, he can heave those water buckets up just like that, and shovel out manure, but I don't have his strength. Doesn't he realize I'm a woman? He didn't even ask me how my back was this morning. He doesn't care, as long as I'm walking around. Well, one of these days, when I can't keep going, he'll be sorry!*

Albert tiptoed out of the bedroom, grinning expectantly. Emma put her fingers to her lips again and motioned toward the bedroom.

Albert put his hand over his mouth and drew his shoulders way up to his earlobes. He snuggled up to her, and she hugged him.

"Come see," she whispered. Mustering enthusiasm, she showed him the wallpaper and box. "I'll make some paste for you," she said, spooning flour into a cup. She stirred it, then demonstrated with a small piece of wallpaper. "You lay it right-side down and put paste on it. Then you lay it on the box, like this, and smooth it down. You can cover the whole thing. Won't that be pretty? I'll give you a wet rag to wipe your fingers on."

While Albert pasted, tongue sticking out of the corner of his mouth, Emma rummaged through her mending basket for a pair of Al's heavy woolen socks.

When Albert started to talk, she quickly put her fingers to her lips.

"I liketa paste!" he whispered.

She flashed him a tiny smile and nodded. When she finished the socks, she rolled them up. "Wipe your fingers, and you can tuck these in Papa's turkey."

"How come you call Papa's knapsack a 'turkey'?"

Emma shrugged. "I don't know who started calling it that. But it kinda looks like a turkey, doesn't it?

He grinned, scampered over to get the socks and put them in the pack, and went back to pasting.

"I'm going to lie down a while," she whispered.

Albert frowned. "Your back hurtin' bad, Mama?"

She nodded. Better that he be concerned about her back than her state of mind.

Ten

Al's Decision

Lying in bed, Emma realized that her back really was hurting. *It could be aching so bad that I won't be able to get up by the time Al comes home,* she thought spitefully. *What would he do if I told him I just couldn't walk? I'd have to limp around and pretend a bit.*

She rolled the thought around a while. It would serve him right. But the money—the horses! No. It was a silly idea. Al had to go back to camp.

For a few moments, Emma enjoyed the luxury of lying still without a single demand on her. Then her thoughts churned again. It was like a little voice taunting, "He doesn't care! He doesn't care about you or the little ones!"

It was true that he hadn't said a word about how she would manage to do the work when he was gone. He hadn't said a thing, except that he had dragged in hay. He never said, "Sure glad Molly's calf didn't come when you were alone." Never said, "Think what could have happened if Fred hadn't dropped that razor, or you hadn't come in when you did?" It was as though it had never happened as far as he was concerned.

A chill still raced through Emma when the scene flashed into her mind. What if Fred *had* been badly cut? He could have bled to death! Why, by the time she could have carried him to Grandpa's house. . . . She groaned and buried her face in the pillow, trying to blot out the horrible scene.

And Al hadn't even mentioned it again!

"Work!" she muttered. "That's all he thinks about." *Ma was so impressed because he was ambitious. Humph! There's more to life than work and earning money. What good is money if one of the little ones gets hurt—or dies?*

I should have thought about all those things before I married him. Someone else would have come along if I had waited. Come to think of it, Al always did take me for granted. That time at the box social, why, he acted like he was doing me a big favor to buy my lunch and eat with me. Nothing shy about him ever. Sometimes I wondered if he came to see me or Ma and Pa. He'd talk and talk with them, and I'd get so mad! He wouldn't pay attention to me until it was time for him to go. Then he'd take my hand, and I'd walk down the drive with him and listen to him tell about his big plans. I never should have let him know I liked him. I could have kept him guessing, but I was afraid he'd turn on his heel and find someone who wouldn't play games with him. I just should have waited. Maybe I'd have seen then what he was really like.

Pretty soon now he'll come stomping in like nothing is wrong. He'll water the stock real quick, have a cup of coffee, and hoist his turkey on his back. Then he'll give me a peck on the cheek, hug the children, and hike off, and probably never even think of us until he's on his way home again next Saturday.

"I don't want to watch him hike off," she continued aloud. "I'll get up and put all his things together and go back to bed."

She had to stop and admire Albert's papering, of course, and then she packed Al's still-damp socks and other clothes. She tied his lunch in a piece of flour sack, mixed more paste for Albert, and went back to bed.

Immediately her thoughts fell back into the same groove. *He's not the man I thought he was, but I'll just have to make the best of it for the children's sake. . . .*

"Papa!" Albert yelled when the door opened and Al stroke in.

Emma didn't move.

When Al shook her shoulder, she still didn't move. "Em! Get up! I gotta talk with you."

She pretended to be asleep.

From the way he was panting, he must have run all the way home. "Emma, get up!" He grabbed her hand and pulled her up.

Frowning, Emma struggled to her feet.

Al put an arm close around her shoulders and led her to the table. Then he leaned over and grasped both of her hands in his cold ones. "Listen!" he gasped. "How'd you like to board the teacher?" He had to catch his breath again. "I talked to Pa and Ma. And to Miss Clark—Jenny. She's willing to come and board here."

Emma's head jerked up. "Board here?"

"Yeah! Look, Em, she'd be here mornings and evenings while you are out doing chores. Noon won't be so bad, 'cause you can get the little ones down for naps and Albert can watch them." He caught his breath again. "And you won't be alone. If anything happened—you needed help or anything—someone else would be here."

Emma's thoughts whirled. "But where . . . where would she sleep?"

"In the loft. I told her what it was like—that it would be cold, but she said she didn't mind. You could leave the door open, so heat would go up."

"But your folks—"

"Pa's sure put out. I think he likes Jenny's company, but Ma never did want to board her. They took her 'cause they were so close to the school. Of course, Ma'll miss the money."

"Money?"

"Sure! She'll pay two dollars a month."

"Two dollars!"

Al patted Emma's cheek. "I want that to be your money to buy dress goods and thread and yarn and whatever you like."

"Two dollars . . . I could buy yards and yards of goods."

"Got any coffee left?"

Emma sprang up so fast she almost knocked the chair over.

"Papa? What's boardin' the teacher mean?" Albert asked, a piece of wallpaper dangling from his fingers.

"That means letting Miss Clark stay here in our house and letting her eat with us. She's going to come and live with us—unless your Mama doesn't want her to."

"Oh, Al, you *know* I want her to come! I'm just so— so surprised."

Emma's hand shook so badly she could hardly fill Al's cup. She put it back on the stove. With her hands over her face she began to cry, huge gulping sobs. Then she felt Al's arms around her.

"Oh, Em, I was about crazy with worry. I didn't know what to do! We need the money so bad, but if anything happened to you or one of the little ones. . . ." His voice broke.

"I—I didn't think you *cared!*" she sobbed.

"Didn't think I cared? I never prayed so hard in my life. I hardly slept at all last night. Then, all of a sudden I remembered us talkin' about Jenny Clark, and how you and the boys liked her. It had to be the answer to my prayers."

There was so much Emma wanted to say, so much she wanted to talk over with Al. But now all she could do was cry out all the tension and anger. He held her close and let her cry while Albert slipped down from the bench and ran in crazy circles yelling, "Miss Clark is gonna live here! Miss Clark is gonna live here!" Fred and Ellie woke up, staggered out, and in moments were running and yelling right with him.

Al and Emma, arms entwined, watched them and laughed. After a long kiss, Al gently released her.

"When's she coming?" Emma asked.

"I told 'em I'd stop by on my way to camp and let 'em know what we decided. Miss Clark said she'd come right away—this evening, if you want her to."

"Oh, my goodness! I have to sweep up there and see that there's enough covers on the bed—and what on earth will I cook for supper?"

She started to go for the broom but came back and leaned her head against Al's shoulder. "I still can't believe she'd really come and stay here. It's so far to walk! Do you think she's doing it 'cause she knows how bad I need her?"

Al shrugged. "Partly, maybe. But it's not easy to live where you aren't welcome, you know."

"I'll try real hard to make it nice for her, but our food is awful plain."

"Don't worry. She's used to plain food." Al gave Emma a quick hug. "I gotta go now and water the stock."

Over and over, as she swept and put clean flour-sack sheets and pillowcases on the bed, Emma wanted to thank God, but she couldn't get the words out. After all the times she had choked back those prayers, He surely was as disappointed and angry with her as she had been with Him.

When she heard Al come in, she scrambled down the narrow stairs. She wanted to creep back into his arms and never let go! And she had thought he didn't care! It didn't matter now that he hadn't told her she had done well. Didn't matter if he *ever* told her.

Ellie, bewildered by all the commotion, clung to Al and cried when he picked her up to say good-bye.

"Papa'll be home soon," he assured her. "You watch by the window. I'll wave at you before I get around the bend."

Only little Georgie was not at the window as Al hiked off.

He was almost to the bend when he wheeled around and hurried back.

Emma bustled to the door. "What did you forget?" she called out. Time was precious. Maybe she could run and get it for him.

He didn't answer. She called again but he still didn't answer—just kept walking all the way to the lean-to door. Then he said, "I just wanted to tell you—those days. . . ." He tapped snow off his boot against the door sill, cleared his throat, and looked up at her, eyes glistening. "Those days last week when you were hurtin' so bad . . . you did real good, Emma."

With a self-conscious wave that was more like a salute, he turned and headed back down the trail.

Emma squeezed her eyes tight a moment and tried to see him again, so she'd remember those tender, glistening eyes. Then she walked out to the lean-to door and waved until he was out of sight.

She wanted to stay out there, hugging his words close, cherishing the moment, but there was work to be done. She gave her eyes a quick dab with her apron and hurried back in.

Eleven

Jenny Moves In

Usually after Al left each Sunday, Emma's throat would ache until she found an opportunity to cry. Not today! She was too excited about Miss Clark's arrival to feel lonesome.

Once Al was out of sight, she hurried back in the house, rolled up the braided rug from beside her bed, and climbed the steep stairs. She put the rug in place and surveyed the little board-lined room. The bare window stared at her. She'd make a curtain as soon as she had time, and put a cushion on the straight-backed chair.

She frowned at the two shelves and wished there were a chest of drawers. Maybe Miss Clark would change her mind when she saw the homemade bed, wooden pegs for clothing, and the unfinished stand with the plain white bowl and pitcher.

Emma fluffed the pillow and straightened the patchwork quilt so the pattern lined up with the edge of the bed. Then, hands on her hips, she sighed and shivered. Even though she had left the door open downstairs, the frost on the window hadn't begun to melt.

Downstairs again, she filled the stove and

pushed the draft wide open. She changed her apron, smoothed her hair, washed the children's faces and hands, changed the baby, and paced from the window to the stove.

"Children! Children, quiet down! You'll scare Miss Clark right back to Grandpa's if she hears you!" Emma yelled over the din.

She glanced at the clock. Al had been gone an hour; Miss Clark could be here any minute. She decided to start supper while she waited.

"Hope she likes potatoes," Emma muttered, as she peeled some for the soup. She shook the coffeepot. Thank goodness—at least two cups' worth left.

"Here she comes!" the boys yelled.

Quickly Emma washed and dried her hands. "Stay in here—it's cold outside," she ordered. She took a deep breath and stepped out into the lean-to.

Miss Clark was stumbling up the bumpy path. "Hello," she called, as soon as she saw Emma.

"Hello!" Emma called back, striving to keep the nervousness out of her voice. "Here! Let me take your bag."

"Oh, no! I'll carry it," Miss Clark insisted. "Your husband told us about your back. Is it better?"

"Oh, yes," Emma assured her. In the dim room she introduced the now quiet children. Little Al smiled, but Fred and Ellie simply stared. Emma motioned to the cradle. "This is Georgie. He's almost three months."

Miss Clark nodded and smiled, but she didn't try to start a conversation with the little ones as she unbuttoned her coat.

Emma tried not to stare at her tiny waist and pretty white blouse. "Will you have a cup of coffee?"

"Well . . . I rarely drink coffee . . . but just this once I will."

Thank goodness, Emma thought as she went to get cups. *There isn't much left.*

"I can't tell you how glad I am that you're going to stay with us. I could hardly believe that you'd be willing to—it's so much farther to walk, and your room will be awfully cold, and we eat plain food and . . ."

Miss Clark chuckled and waved her slender hand as she sat down with a swish of her long black skirt. "Believe me, none of those things compare with—" She stopped, mid-sentence, and glanced toward the children.

Emma smiled and nodded. "I know," she said.

Miss Clark returned her smile and nod. They both knew Grandma Verleger.

Ellie clamored to get up on Emma's lap, and the boys hovered nearby.

"I hope you like potato soup."

"Oh, I do! Please don't worry about the food. Give me enough milk to drink, an egg for breakfast, plenty of potatoes and bread, and I'm happy. Of course, it would be nice to have a raw onion sandwich when I get home from school each afternoon."

"Raw onion sandwich?"

"Oh, yes! Haven't you ever eaten one? My grandmother used to say it wards off colds, but I eat them because they taste so good!"

Emma chuckled. "Well, we have plenty of onions—and bread."

At the supper table Emma was grateful that shyness kept the children quiet. Miss Clark said the soup was delicious, and she smiled so openly at Emma that her nervousness vanished. Emma found herself freely asking questions.

"I know you come from out East, but I don't know where."

"I was born in Connecticut, but I lived most of my life near Boston."

"Why did you come here? Didn't you like it there?"

Miss Clark chuckled. "Oh, I liked it there well enough, but when I heard of the opportunity to teach in the Northwoods, I felt an excitement that's hard to explain. I knew I had to come. I had been praying for the Lord's will for my life, and I knew this was where He wanted me."

Emma was both startled and happy to hear this frank statement of faith in the Lord's guidance. The only person she knew who came close to talking about her faith like that was Kate. But in spite of her gladness that Miss Clark was a special kind of Christian, Emma felt uncomfortable—as though Miss Clark might somehow know that Emma wasn't on speaking terms with God at the moment.

Quickly she asked, "Were you ever in New York City?"

Miss Clark nodded.

"What's it like?"

"Oh, it's noisy and crowded. I like to see the skyline from a distance, but I don't like to be in it. I enjoy nature more than what man has built."

"The only city I've been in is Oshkosh—and Phillips, of course, but that's just a town. Do you have brothers and sisters?"

Miss Clark finished her soup before she replied. "I have two sisters—both married—and a brother who is younger."

"And your parents?"

"They still live near Boston. I wonder how they are," she said pensively. "It takes so long for our letters to get through. Someone usually goes to the post office on Mondays. I'll have to stop at Grandpa Verleger's tomorrow night and see if I have any mail."

"Al said Grandpa didn't like it much that you were moving here."

Miss Clark sighed, "I'm sorry about that. He's a nice old man. I know he wanted me to come for your sake, but still it hurt his feelings to think I'd leave."

"He'll get over it."

"I suppose he will. But he warned me not to come crying to him if I got in trouble." Her brow furrowed. "That puzzles me. What kind of trouble could I have? He said he didn't mean that the two of us would have trouble getting along."

Emma shrugged. "Who knows? He has a way of looking at the dark side of things."

They talked a while longer and then made plans for the morning. Miss Clark said she wanted to leave the house by seven.

A long while after Miss Clark—Jenny—had gone to bed, Emma was still awake, thinking over all the things they had talked about. They had decided to call each other by their first names, except when the children were around. Emma said it wouldn't be proper for them to call her anything but Miss Clark.

It had surprised Emma to learn that Jenny was twenty-eight—five years her senior. *She looks younger than I do, and she's so pretty*, Emma thought, as she recalled Jenny's slim waist, glowing red hair piled high, and long graceful fingers. And their differences went far beyond the obvious physical ones.

Jenny's family had been in America since before the Revolutionary War; Emma's parents, only since the War Between the States. Jenny had grown up in Connecticut, lived near Boston, and visited New York, Philadelphia, and even Washington, D.C. Except for her move from Oshkosh at age ten, Emma had never traveled outside a thirty-mile radius of Ogema, Wisconsin.

Jenny had gone to school until she was eighteen; Emma, only as far as the third reader. Jenny had read more books than Emma knew existed; Emma had actually never read a complete book.

The wonderful part about it was that, in spite of their differences and Jenny's advantages, Jenny didn't make her feel inferior. It wasn't so much what she *said* that kept Emma from feeling like an unlearned farm woman, but the way she looked at her—with approval, bordering on admiration. Emma couldn't even remember the color of her eyes—only that they held a rare warmth that melted Emma's apprehension.

Emma saw, too, that they had many things in common: their mutual love of nature and children, the pleasure they found in accomplishment, their desire for everyone to be loving and kind.

A shiver of excitement made Emma cuddle deeper into the covers. Questions swarmed into her mind. Jenny had to be the answer to Al's prayers—maybe even the answer to hers. But the thought of God banished the excitement and left only regret.

Even in the darkness she wanted to hide her face when she thought about how angry she had been at God for not helping her. How many times she had felt this way as a child, when she had sassed her mother or disobeyed her. She could see her mother working, tight-lipped and grim, refusing to speak to her for hours, even days after Emma had misbehaved.

She sighed and groaned. She didn't blame God for being angry and disgusted with her. Here He had been planning all along to send her help—help for all winter, not just for a day or two, but she had insisted on help *right now!* She rolled over, trying to get away from the echo of her impatient words and the memory of all the times she had doubted and refused to pray.

When the baby cried at five, Emma didn't want to move but, remembering that cold room upstairs, she hurried to fix the fire. Her excitement returned with the dawn, and she chattered happily through breakfast, thankful that shyness still kept the children comfortably quiet.

Jenny was hardly out of the house, though, before they reverted to their usual noisy selves.

When Emma watered the cattle at noon, she realized

her back didn't hurt nearly as much as yesterday. Gratitude flooded through her. While the little ones napped, she rolled out molasses cookies and let Albert help cut them with a scalloped cutter Kate had given her. If only she could tell Kate all that had happened. Kate would love Jenny!

"Oh my, you look tired!" Emma said as Jenny sagged into the rocker when she got home Monday night.

"I'll get used to the walk," Jenny assured her. "There's a lot of snow. I tried to brush the snow off my skirt, but it was wet until noon."

"It's probably wet now. Can I get you a dry skirt?"

Jenny jumped up. "Oh, no! I'll change. Is it all right if I hang my wet skirt behind the stove?"

Oh dear, Emma thought when Jenny went up to change. *I hope we don't have another snowstorm.*

After Jenny had changed her skirt, she ate her onion sandwich and the children ate cookies. They showed her their treasures: pictures, pretty stones, Ellie's red ribbon. Emma let them chatter. She'd have her turn to talk after the little ones were in bed.

At suppertime, Emma saw that Jenny was waiting for her to ask the blessing, but she busied herself getting Ellie settled. Surely Jenny would simply bow her own head and pray silently, as she had done last night and this morning.

Then Albert piped up, "When Papa's home, *we* pray, too."

Emma felt her cheeks flush. She didn't dare look at Jenny. Then Albert began to chatter, and the uncomfortable moment passed. Jenny, she noticed, bowed her head a moment before she ate.

Later, when the children were in bed, Emma made up for her silence. She told Jenny about her fears for the children, how she had yearned for someone to talk to, how she missed Kate and her parents, and many other things. She carefully avoided talking about her discord with God.

All too soon the clock struck nine, and the two women reluctantly prepared for bed. Emma filled the stove. "I hope you won't be cold tonight. I'll try to keep the fire going."

"I'll be fine," Jenny assured her, filling the china pitcher with hot water. "I'm so glad I'm here. We're going to have a wonderful winter, Emma. You have such a keen mind—I can't wait to see you enjoy some good books. I'll read to you while you knit or sew, if you like."

"I *would* like that!" Emma exclaimed.

It was comforting to hear the floor squeak above her as Jenny prepared for bed. *Surely tonight I'll go right to sleep.* Snuggled in bed, Emma tried to think about all the pleasant things they'd talked about. But, once again, guilt-ridden thoughts plagued her. When sleep finally came, she dreamed that Jesus was frowning at her.

Twelve

Raw Onions and Green Wood

"When will Miss Clark be home?" the children asked on Tuesday, more times than Emma could count. She didn't blame them. She was eager, too, for the light and laughter that Jenny brought with her.

Gratitude welled up in her as she shaped bread dough into loaves. She wanted to thank God for sending Jenny, but she could still see Jesus frowning at her as He had in her dream. Over and over she pushed aside those troublesome thoughts and concentrated on the new things she had heard from Jenny. But no matter how hard she tried, regret clung like a bad taste in her mouth.

When Jenny got home, the fragrant brown-crusted bread was cooling on Emma's whitest dish towel. Only her best would do now, as she saw everything through Jenny's eyes.

"Yum . . . the bread smells good," Jenny said as she made her onion sandwich.

Emma and the children joined her at the table— with bread and syrup.

Jenny told them how the school children had sung song after song that morning, and how well the little ones were beginning to read. Even Ernie, who had tried her patience almost to the limit all winter, had done neat sums on his slate.

Albert wrinkled his nose. "What's a slate?"

Jenny flashed him a smile. "I have one of my own at Verlegers', Albert. Instead of telling you about it, I'll stop by and pick it up tomorrow night, and you can use it." She turned to Emma. "I need to bring more of my things over here. Grandpa said there was no hurry, but I know Grandma!"

When the children ran off to play, Jenny said, "Wait 'til you see what I brought for us to read tonight!" Eyes twinkling, she pulled a book out of her school bag and handed it to Emma.

"*Little Women*," Emma read.

"It's about four sisters. I read it twice a long while ago, but I don't mind reading it again."

Reverently Emma fingered the pages. "My goodness, it's long. It'll take us all winter."

"I thought you could read some during the day, and we'll pick up at night where you leave off. I don't mind."

"But my work! My knitting! I can't waste time reading!"

"Emma, reading isn't a waste of time. Some of the most important things in life are the ones we can't see!"

"But I have work to get done."

"You will. You'll be surprised how fast you'll work, when you have a reason to get it done—something to look forward to."

After supper Jenny began to clear the table, but Emma said, "No, you rest. You look all worn out."

For a moment Emma thought Jenny might burst into tears. "Want to tell me about it?" she asked gently, as she filled the dish pan with hot water.

Jenny nodded. "First of all, I couldn't get the fire started this morning. There's so little kindling wood left, and I've been trying not to use much. But the wood is so green, it just lies there and smokes. We had to wear our coats until almost noon. I'd have the children get up and stomp their feet now and then to warm up." Her face brightened. "You should have heard them!"

Emma chuckled. "I can imagine. And you must have been frozen stiff. When you were at Grandpa's, did you used to start the fire earlier and then go back to the warm house?"

"Oh, yes. Sometimes I'd make several trips. The room would be quite warm by the time school started." She sighed. "I'd better leave half an hour earlier tomorrow morning."

Emma washed the last dish and poured out the water. "About the kindling. . . . Who cut wood for the school this year?"

"Mr. Schuft."

Emma groaned. "I might have known. You could send a note home with young Herman, and tell Mr. Schuft you need more kindling."

"I did, last week. He wrote back that I shouldn't have used it like firewood. He said the school doesn't have any more money for wood this year, and he isn't bringing any more."

While Emma did chores that evening, she fretted about Jenny in that cold schoolroom. By the time she came in from the barn, Jenny had started getting the children ready for bed. When the little ones were tucked in, Emma's knitting needles clicked faster than ever as she listened to Jenny read.

Once Jenny stopped for breath, and Emma said, "Jo is my sister Gustie all over again—always doing something unladylike."

"How many sisters do you have?" Jenny asked.

"Two now. My sister Anne died."

"Oh, I'm sorry. Do the others live near here?"

"Winnie lives over in Knox, about five or six miles

away, but Gustie lives up in Ashland. I was so sad when she got married and moved way up there. I don't get to see much of Winnie, either."

"So you were the last one married. You must have been lonesome."

Emma nodded. "I sure was. I know Ma must be lonesome now, with all of us gone. Of course Walter and Dick are still home, and she has my sister Anne's daughter, little Anne. And Pa. But Pa doesn't talk to Ma much. I can't ever remember him asking her opinion about anything."

Jenny put the book down on her lap.

Emma continued. "That's what I especially liked about Al . . . uh . . . Mr. Verleger. He *talked* to me. He asked me what I thought about things."

"Where did you meet him?"

"Right in my home. He came to talk to my father."

"And then?"

Emma's face flushed. "Well, I took notice of him that day, but I wasn't sure he noticed me. He had, though. A few weeks later he appeared and said he had come to see *me!*"

"How long was it, then, before you got married?"

"About a year later. We were married the first of July."

"Did you have a big wedding?

Emma looked puzzled. "A big wedding?"

"Yes," Jenny continued brightly. "Did you have lots of bridesmaids and a big reception?"

"Reception? Well, up here no one makes much fuss about weddings. The couple just goes wherever they can find a justice of the peace or a minister, and they get married. Sometimes there's a square dance in their honor."

"Oh," Jenny said softly. She sounded so disappointed that Emma hurriedly explained.

"You see, people here just don't have money for anything that isn't really necessary. I wanted so much to have a minister marry us, but we would have had to go somewhere on the train and stay overnight, and that would have cost a lot. What little Al had, we needed for nails and window glass and things for this house and a cow and an ox and seed. . . . I didn't have any money at all, because I'd always worked at home. Of course, Ma gave me lots of things to get started."

Jenny hesitated a moment. Then she asked, "But you were happy on your wedding day?"

Emma's face brightened. "Oh, yes! We were happy. We walked to Ogema to the justice of the peace, Mr. Morgan, and we laughed and talked and—" She laughed. "Well, you know what young couples do."

Jenny joined her laughter.

"Well," Emma said, "on the way back we stopped at Pearson's Lake and went for a boat ride." She leaned back and closed her eyes. "I'll never forget how beautiful it was. I don't know what was more beautiful—the white birch and evergreen trees along the curving shore line, or Al's big, strong arms rowing that boat like it was no effort at all. He sang some, too. He's got a real good voice. I remember he sang, 'The Maple on the Hill,' 'cause he knew that was my favorite."

"And then you walked all the way back here? It must be ten miles from Ogema!"

"More like thirteen. But we were used to walking, and just being together made it seem no distance at all."

"And you didn't have any celebration?"

"No. Al kinda wanted a square dance, but he knew I don't enjoy them. We were too busy just getting down to plain living for a lot of fuss."

Jenny sat quietly a moment, and Emma began knitting again. "Shall I finish reading this chapter and stop for tonight?" Jenny asked. "Morning comes fast!" She read a few more pages and paused. "Why don't you read the last page of this chapter, Emma?"

Reluctantly Emma laid down her knitting. She hadn't read two sentences when she came to a word she didn't know. Patiently Jenny leaned over and helped her sound it out. Whew! Emma pronounced the word and read the rest of the page as rapidly as she could while Jenny's onion breath engulfed her.

As she undressed later, smiling to herself in the dark, she planned how she'd tell Al about it. "I didn't know I could read that fast," she'd tell him. It always felt so good to laugh together.

On Wednesday, Emma thought a lot about the sisters in the book. When the children napped, she read a few more pages, but it wasn't nearly as much fun to read it herself as it had been to listen to Jenny. She put the book down with a sigh. How did Jenny learn to read without ever stumbling over a word?

Each time Emma went to do chores knowing the children were safe with Jenny, her thankfulness grew. Wednesday night she nearly wept with relief when she looked out of the barn window at the pale light from the cabin and thought of the children laughing and secure while she worked. *I don't deserve it. But will it last? Maybe she'll have to go back to Grandpa's, if she keeps having trouble getting the fire started.*

When Emma came in, Jenny had the children ready for bed. She was sitting in the rocker with Ellie in one arm, Georgie in the other, and the boys at her feet, singing a silly little song Emma had never heard. *I can't wait to tell Al how happy the little ones are,* she thought as she washed her hands.

When the children were in bed, Jenny sat down close to the lamp with *two* books. "Emma, I've been thinking. Wouldn't it be good if we read the Bible, too, each evening?"

"Yes . . . Yes, I suppose so," Emma faltered.

"Would you like to begin with the Gospels, or go on to one of the Epistles?"

"I—I don't know." Emma lowered her eyes. "I mean, I don't know what they are."

"The Gospels are Matthew, Mark, Luke, and John—the story of Jesus' life here on earth, His crucifixion and resurrection," Jenny explained without a hint of reproach in her voice. "The Epistles are letters that the Apostles wrote to the early churches."

Emma still didn't look up. "I don't know much about the Bible. The only time we went to church was a few times when we lived in Phillips and, before I was ten, when we lived in Oshkosh." She sighed. "I tried to read it once, but I never got farther than Numbers. It was hard to read that tiny print by lamp light . . . and all those funny names."

"We'll read from the New Testament. That's easier, and there aren't so many names. We'll find things that will mean something to us for right now—things we can *use!* Wait'll you hear!" Jenny flipped through the pages, holding the Bible close to the light. "Listen to this, from Paul's letter to the Philippians, chapter four, verse four: 'Rejoice in the Lord alway: and again I say, Rejoice. Let your moderation be known unto all men. The Lord is at hand. Be careful for nothing; but in every thing by prayer and supplication with thanksgiving let your requests be made known unto God. And the peace of God, which passeth all understanding, shall keep your hearts and minds through Christ Jesus.'" Jenny smiled at Emma. "Isn't that beautiful?"

Emma looked puzzled. "Will you read that first part again—about not being careful about anything? I don't understand."

"Let's see. That's verse six: 'Be careful for nothing, but in every thing by prayer and supplication with thanksgiving let your requests be made known unto God.'"

"Why aren't we supposed to do things carefully?"

"It doesn't mean that. It means we aren't supposed to

be full of care—anxious—about anything. We're not supposed to worry."

"Oh, my goodness! I didn't know that!"

Jenny's eyes glowed. "Isn't that wonderful. We don't *have* to be concerned and fearful. All we have to do is bring our worry to God in prayer!"

Emma didn't answer. That sounded real nice, for people God wasn't angry with. "Did you go to church a lot?" she asked, trying to change the subject.

"Oh, yes! Sunday morning, Sunday night, Wednesday night. And sometimes we had prayer meetings on Friday nights."

"Prayer meetings?"

"Didn't you ever go to a prayer meeting?"

Emma shook her head. "Didn't you get tired of going to church?"

"When I was little I did, and when I was in my teens I didn't want to go to church at all. I wanted to live my life the way I wanted to live it, and I was afraid if I let God take it over, He'd take away all my fun."

"What happened? Did He?"

Jenny laughed. "No. He certainly didn't. It seemed that during those years when I was holding out, the harder I tried to have fun and do things my way, the worse I felt. I tried to act like I was happy, but I wasn't fooling anybody. I found out later that my grandparents, my parents, and especially my brother Peter, were praying for me all the while. Finally, one Sunday night, I started to cry in church. I couldn't stop until I told God I was tired of trying to run my own life, and if He wanted me He could be boss—I mean the Lord of my life."

"Were you ever sorry you gave in?"

Jenny beamed at Emma. "Never! He didn't take my fun away. I found out that God never takes anything away, unless He replaces it with something much better. The things I thought were fun weren't important anymore. I started to like different things."

"I gave my life to Jesus when I was a little girl in Osh-kosh."

Jenny squeezed Emma's hand. "Oh, Emma! I'm so glad you did."

Jenny closed the Bible and began to read from *Little Women*, but Emma wasn't concentrating. She was trying to imagine Jenny fighting God, but all she could see was Jenny the way she was now, her eyes full of love.

Thursday was a long day. Albert waited impatiently for Miss Clark to bring the slate. Even though there was a cold wind, Emma finally bundled him up and let him play outside while he waited. "Don't go any farther than the bend!" she warned him.

Of course Jenny was later than usual, because she had to stop at Grandpa Verleger's to get the slate. Albert must have run from the house to the bend fifty times before he came puffing in behind Miss Clark.

"See," Jenny explained when they got their coats off, "I've printed your name on the top. Now you can print it below."

She handed him the slate pencil and winked at Emma. "That'll keep him busy," she whispered. "Fred! Ellie! Come here! Tell me what you did today. Can you sing the song we sang last night?"

How did I ever manage alone? Emma asked herself as she put wood in the stove.

When the children were in bed, Jenny read a chapter from Matthew. They talked about what she had read for a few minutes. Then she said "Do you mind if I don't read any more tonight? My throat is a little sore." Jenny cleared her throat. "I would like to talk a while, though."

"Did you get the fire started faster this morning?" Emma asked.

"A little faster, but the room was still terribly cold when I had a visitor—Mrs. Gross."

"Oh, dear!"

"She stormed in and shook her fist at me! You know how big she is. I was so shocked; I guess I just stood there with my mouth open."

"What was she mad about?"

"The cold schoolroom. She reminded me that her husband is on the school board, and he'd see that I got fired if I didn't have it warm by the time the children got there tomorrow."

"Did you tell her about the kindling and green wood?"

Jenny shook her head. "I didn't have a chance. She shouted some more and stomped out." Jenny's voice was soft when she continued. "I've been praying that Grandpa Verleger will have a change of heart and help me. He has plenty of kindling wood. He could give some to the school." She smiled shyly. "I'm even praying that he'll offer to start the fire for me. He's always up early."

Later, snuggled deep under the covers, Jenny's words came back to Emma. She hadn't wanted to discourage Jenny, but Emma couldn't imagine Grandpa giving kindling wood to the school, much less starting the fire. *I'd never even think of praying for something so impossible. Hope she isn't too disappointed when God doesn't do it.*

When the clock struck ten, she was still worrying. Then she remembered what Jenny had read about not worrying, but praying instead. It didn't help *her* a bit. How long would it take, Emma wondered, until she felt free to pray again? The only comfort she could find was knowing that Al would be home in two days. She hugged his pillow and fell asleep.

Thirteen

Unspoken Prayers

It was Fred who discovered the winter wonderland Friday morning. "Mama, yook!" he called. "The trees is all fwowered!"

Emma chuckled as she peered out of the window where Fred had melted the frost with his hand. "It sure is!" She beckoned to Jenny. "Fred says it's 'floured' out there. He sees me sift flour when I bake."

Jenny took a peek and said, "Oh, let's go look!"

She pulled on her coat and helped Fred with his, while Emma threw a shawl around herself and Ellie.

At the door of the lean-to, they huddled a moment in rapt silence.

"It's so beautiful. . . ." Jenny whispered. "I've never seen frost like this before. It's a fairyland!" She beamed an ecstatic smile at Emma.

"It is beautiful," Emma said, returning Jenny's smile as best she could. But as she turned to go in, she saw a hint of disappointment dim Jenny's smile. She had realized that Emma wasn't sharing her ecstasy.

Later, as Emma washed breakfast dishes, she

thought, *What's the matter with me? I had that same cover-on-the-jar feeling. My eyes tell me it's beautiful, but the sight doesn't make me feel good down inside.*

All week she had tried to ignore the emptiness she felt in spite of all the good things that had happened.

Carefully she listed as many blessings as she could think of:

Al really cared about the children. He had proved that.

The children loved Jenny and were safe while she did chores.

It was exciting and fun to have Jenny around—in spite of her onion breath.

Al was earning money for the team and other needs.

They were all healthy.

It would soon be spring.

Her back was almost well.

But, instead of brightening her mood, the reminder of all the things she had to be thankful for made her feel guiltier than ever. *You should be so happy!* she scolded herself.

Dishes done, Emma put water in the small tub to bathe Georgie. When she splashed water on his tummy, he laughed out loud and waved his chubby little arms.

"You are so precious," she told him. Holding his wiggly little body close in the towel, she recalled a conversation with Jenny yesterday.

Emma had confessed that she felt a twinge of envy when she watched Jenny hike off for school in the morning, and Jenny had laughed and said, "Isn't that the way! The grass is always greener on the other side of the fence. I walk away thinking how nice it must be to stay in the cozy warm house with your *own* children and look forward to seeing your man every weekend."

She sighed longingly. "I'll never forget Mr. Verleger's voice when he told us how concerned he was about leaving you alone with the children, and how proud he was of how you had managed those days after you hurt your back." She lowered her voice almost to a whisper. "I thought, *If a man ever loves me like that, I'll be completely happy!*"

"I *will* be happy," Emma said aloud now, as she patted Georgie dry. Determinedly she set her mind on all she could do to make the days Al was home as pleasant as possible.

Emma heard Jenny coughing when she came home from school before she even opened the door. *Oh, dear! That cold room! What if she gets pneumonia?* F e a r swept over her. *Maybe she will have to go back to Grandpa's.*

"I sound worse than I feel," Jenny insisted when Emma asked about her health. "The weather will change. We're due for a thaw. That will help."

Sure, and you'll have wet, cold feet instead of cold, wet feet, Emma thought. But she mustered a smile as she sliced bread.

"Don't look so glum!" Jenny said cheerily as she warmed her hands over the stove. "Grandpa's going to change his mind and help me. You'll see!"

Emma bit her tongue and didn't reply. *Sometimes she acts like a child. A person has to face things as they are, not go on dreaming they're going to change.*

"Would you like to take a bath down here in my bedroom where it's warmer?" Emma asked Jenny as she dished up their supper. "You can use the big washtub."

"That would be lovely. Grandma Verleger informed me that a sponge bath was good enough, so I haven't had a tub bath since fall." Quickly she added, "I'll watch the little ones when I'm done, and you can have your bath."

Of course the children clamored for baths when Emma carried the tub into the bedroom and Jenny began to fill it with water.

"Not tonight," Emma said, "I can't heat enough water for all of us. Tomorrow night is your bath night."

Even though she had a scant four inches of water in the tub and had to sit with her knees up to her chin, it felt good to wring the washcloth and let the warm water run down her body while the children squealed delightedly with Jenny in the other room.

If only Al could be home tonight.

By Saturday morning, Albert could print his name without a pattern to look at. He danced around with the slate, chanting, "I can't wait till Papa comes home! I can't wait till Papa comes home!"

He was making too much noise to hear Jenny ask Emma if she could take him along to Grandpa Verleger's to get the rest of her things.

When Emma agreed, Jenny added, "I'll wait until Fred and Ellie are asleep. Fred's little legs are just too short to keep up with us."

"Are you sure you should go out with that cough? Maybe if you stayed in until Monday, you'd—"

"Emma! I'm all right! Stop fussing over me." Her voice softened. "I think that goose grease you gave me last night really helped."

Jenny and Albert had been gone about half an hour when Emma heard footsteps. They couldn't be back already.

There in the doorway stood Al, a big grin on his face.

Emma flashed him a smile. "Sh-h. The little ones are asleep, and Jenny took Albert with her to get the rest of her things."

He pulled off his knapsack, hung up his coat, and rubbed his hands over the stove. "So it's 'Jenny,' is it? Sounds like you two are kinda chummy."

"Oh, yes. But I don't call her Jenny in front of the children," Emma assured him as she put water in the coffeepot.

Before she could add the coffee, he wrapped his arms around her and kissed her soundly. "Oh, Emma, it's good to be home! You feeling all right?"

She nodded, still clinging to him in spite of the camp odor in his shirt.

He released her gently, knowing she didn't appreciate his whiskers. "I'll shave while the coffee cooks," he whispered. "How long have they been gone?"

Emma glanced at the clock. "Close to an hour. They could be back any minute, so you can get that gleam out of your eye!"

Al grinned at her, shrugged, and started mixing his shaving soap. "So, how is it going with Miss Clark—Jenny?"

"Good! Really good. She has a special way with the children, and she and I get along fine. She reads out loud while I knit or sew in the evening. I like that. But I don't like it when she wants me to read a page or two before we stop."

"What's wrong with you reading a little?"

Emma giggled. "It isn't the reading I mind, even if I do stumble over a lot of words. But every night when she comes home from school, she makes herself a big, raw onion sandwich. . . . So when she leans over to help me sound out words . . . whew!"

Al's grin spread, and he choked back his laughter so he wouldn't wake the little ones.

Emma made a face. "She said her grandmother told her it would ward off colds. That I believe! No one'll get close enough to give her one."

"Well, if that's all . . ."

"What do you mean, 'if that's all'," Emma said in mock indignation. "You should have her breathing down *your* neck with onion breath!"

He raised his eyebrows. "If Jenny breathed down my neck, I wouldn't even notice the onion breath," he teased.

"She is pretty, isn't she," Emma said wistfully.

Al looked up from mixing his shaving lather. "Yeah, she's pretty all right. I don't mind looking at her. But I don't mind looking at you, either."

He took two long steps toward her, tilted her chin up with one finger, and kissed her tenderly. "I love *you*," he said and stepped back to the washstand.

"It's a wonder the roof stays on!" Emma said to Jenny, as Al rough-housed with the children while they cooked supper.

Of course, he had to admire Albert's printing.

"I'm gonna yearn, too," Fred assured him, his blond locks bobbing as he nodded.

When Al began to pray at the table, Fred giggled and poked Albert. Al stopped and gave him a stern look, and Fred's smile vanished. He folded his hands.

When Al had finished, he looked sternly at Fred again and said, "Is that the way you behave while your Mama prays when I'm gone?"

Emma's heart all but stopped.

Fred merely shook his head, and no one said a word until Al started talking to Jenny. "How do you like the Northwoods?"

"It's different in many ways," she answered, "and I miss my family and friends, but I like the clean air and the tall pine trees, and people here have been friendly."

"And the school?"

She hesitated a moment before she answered, "It's certainly a challenge. I first taught in city schools."

Al chuckled. "It *must* be a challenge. Are the children different from the ones out East?"

"No, not much different." She toyed with her fork a moment and said, "I can't seem to get close to the children here. When I lean over to help them with their work, they pull away from me."

"The children out East didn't do that?"

"No, they didn't."

Al shot a quick glance at Emma and continued. "Emma tells me you're fond of raw onion sandwiches. Did you always eat them?"

"Oh, no! My mother abhorred them, but here . . ."

A smile twitched at the corners of Emma's mouth. Al gave Jenny a sidelong glance and kept eating.

For a little while everyone was quiet, except for Emma's encouraging Ellie to drink her milk.

Suddenly Jenny dropped her fork, put her hand over her mouth, and said, "You mean . . . you mean . . .?"

Al grinned.

Much to Emma's relief, Jenny laughed. "You mean those poor children are trying to get away from my onion breath?"

Emma could feel her face growing warm.

"Emma! You, too! Why didn't you tell me?"

"I didn't know how. I didn't know the children were having the same trouble, or I might have said something."

Jenny picked up her fork and shook it as she spoke. "Well, I know one thing! I have eaten my last raw onion sandwich."

"Well, ladies," Al said abruptly, "you ready for some music?"

Jenny's eyebrows shot up. "Music?"

Emma told her that Al played the accordion, and Jenny clapped her hands. "That's wonderful! I haven't heard music for so long, except for our singing at school." She turned to Emma. "I'll be glad to do the dishes, if you want to help with the chores."

Emma nodded. "Thanks! We can get done much faster. When I come in, I'll bathe the children and we'll have *music!*"

"Quite a change from a week ago, huh?" Al called from the other end of the barn as Emma milked Molly.

"I've had a lot of prayers answered, but never in a better way than this one. Sure makes me want to keep prayin'!"

Emma didn't answer. *Good thing he feels like praying. He's going to have to pray for both of us. I better tell him about the fire-starting problem, so he can pray about that.*

When Al was working closer to her, she said, "I don't know how long Jenny will be able to stay, though. She's having a terrible time getting the fire started at school, and she has to be in that cold room all that while—and then sleep in our cold upstairs besides."

"Doesn't she know how to start a fire? Shouldn't take that long to warm up a schoolroom."

"Oh, she knows how to start a fire, but there's hardly any kindling left, and Mr. Schuft says he isn't bringing any more. She took a few shavings from here, but she can't carry much. I know there isn't any money to pay for more wood this year. Mrs. Gross came one morning and threatened to have Jenny fired if that schoolroom wasn't warm when school started in the morning. If only Grandpa would help her. And he has a whole pile of kindling; I wish he'd give some to the school."

"He's not likely to do that. He sure was put out when she moved. Say, maybe that's what he meant by her having trouble! I never thought of the fire."

"It would help so much if she could still run over there to the warm house until the fire got going." She was about to tell Al about Jenny's prayers but decided not to. It would be just like Al to agree with Jenny that God would change Grandpa's mind. Then they'd both be disappointed.

"Maybe I better go and talk to Pa tomorrow."

"I don't think Jenny would want you to. Besides, I can't remember anyone ever getting your Pa to change his mind."

"Yeah, I guess you're right."

When they got back to the house, Jenny not only had the dishes done, but she was just finishing the children's baths.

Eyes riveted on Al's every move, the children watched him take down the accordion and unlatch it. But when his starting warm-up chords leaped into the air, Fred and Ellie's attention turned to Albert who crouched, taut as a runner waiting for the starting signal.

As Al began to squeeze out a tune, Albert gave a whoop and sprang into his own version of the polka, immediately followed by Fred and Ellie.

Georgie sat on Emma's lap, transfixed. When Emma laughed at the children's comical attempts to polka, he swiveled his round-eyed gaze to her face.

"Georgie dance, too," she shouted in his ear, bouncing him on her knee. He rewarded her with a bare-gummed smile.

When Al switched to a slower tempo, Emma leaned back, closed her eyes, and drank in the soothing melody. Then she opened her eyes and flashed a smile at Jenny.

Jenny smiled back, but it was plain to see she was fighting tears.

Emma pretended not to notice. When she caught Al's eye, he raised his eyebrows questioningly. Emma replied with a shrug.

When the tune ended, Al got up, took a drink of water, and put wood in the stove.

Emma leaned toward Jenny. "Are you homesick?"

Jenny shook her head and then nodded. "I guess. It's just that I never . . ."

But before she could finish, Al came back and sat down with his long arm draped over the accordion. "I know I'm not much of a musician," he said with a chuckle, "but I never made anyone cry before."

Jenny smiled. "Oh, I like your playing. I really do. It's just that it's so—so different. When you said music, I thought of my family gathered around the organ singing hymns."

"What were some of them?" Emma asked softly.

"Oh, 'Blessed Assurance, Jesus is Mine' and 'Just As I Am Without One Plea'."

"We know those, don't we Al?"

He nodded and tried to play "Blessed Assurance," but there were so many sour notes they all laughed. "I guess I'll have to practice that. Let's just try it without the accordion." He threw back his head and began to sing. Emma and Jenny joined him with their high, sweet voices, but Jenny ended up singing the second verse alone, because Al and Emma didn't know all the words.

"I think I know all of 'Just As I Am'," Emma said, and took the lead.

When they finished, Al asked, "Do you know 'Jesus Lover of My Soul'?"

Jenny began to sing and the others joined her.

The children sat on the floor in rapt attention. Emma smiled at Al, who had noticed Jenny's radiant face just as she had. *I wish this moment could last forever,* she thought.

The clock struck eight. "Time for bed, *Kinder!*"

"Aw . . .!" they protested.

"Could we sing 'Savior Breathe an Evening Blessing'?" Emma asked. "Do you know it, Jenny?"

Jenny smiled and began softly singing as Al and Emma harmonized.

Now it was Emma's turn to blink hard as the song ended, and she laid sleeping Georgie in the cradle.

Eyes glowing, Jenny quickly said good night and went upstairs.

"Into bed now!" Al ordered. As the children scampered off, he smiled down at Emma.

She leaned her head on his chest and sighed as his arms enfolded her. "Let's do that more often," she whispered.

Sunday afternoon Emma finished packing Al's clothes to take back to camp. She glanced at the clock. Only a little over an hour and he'd have to leave again. It seemed as though he had just gotten home. Where had the day gone? Al had worked in the barn a good share of the time, the boys with him. Jenny had insisted on helping Emma wherever she could.

Emma smiled as she watched Jenny carefully get up from the rocker with baby George in her arms and put him in his cradle.

Ellie tottered out of the bedroom, rubbing her eyes. "Papa? Papa?"

"Papa's outside," Emma assured her, hugging her close and kissing her warm cheek.

When Emma put her down, Jenny whispered, "Would it be all right if I took her for a sleigh ride? There's hardly any wind."

"I suppose so. But shouldn't you stay in with that cough?"

Jenny shook her head. "I'm fine. It's so nice outside. The boys can come, too."

Emma bundled Ellie up, and Jenny carried her out and put her on the little wooden sled. She called to the boys, who were chasing each other around the woodshed, and they all started down the road.

"I think Jenny took the children just to give us a little time to talk," Emma said, when Al came in and sat down to have a cup of coffee.

He stirred his coffee thoughtfully. "Maybe I should have gone to see Pa today about helping her."

Emma shook her head. "Wouldn't have done any good."

Al chuckled. "You're right."

"Do you think Mr. Gross will get the school board riled up about the cold schoolroom?"

Al shrugged. "Wouldn't take much to get the Schufts to side with them."

Emma went to get hot coffee.

They were silent a moment; then Emma said, "I feel like I'm walking on eggs—any day she'll decide it's too hard and move back to Grandpa's."

"No sense worrying," Al said. He told Emma about the stock and what she should do while he was gone.

All too soon Jenny and the children burst in the door, rosy-cheeked and breathless.

Ellie, who had been all smiles, burst into tears when Al put on his coat and shouldered his pack.

While he tried to comfort her, Jenny pulled Emma aside. "I'll watch the children if you'd like to walk a ways with him."

"Oh! Yes!" Emma said and went to put on her overshoes and coat.

They walked in silence, Emma dreading the moment when Al would have to go on and she would be left to turn back to the house. "It'll be pitch dark before you get to the train," she said.

"That doesn't bother me. There'll be four or five of us hiking together before we get to Ogema." He looked up at the clear sky and the almost full moon. "See! There will be moonlight."

Emma's teeth chattered. "It's getting awfully cold!"

"I'm not cold. You're just not used to being outdoors like I am." He put his arm around her. "You're shivering. You'd better go back now."

He pulled her close and she clung to him, cheek against his rough wool coat. She lifted her face for his kiss.

"Hurry back in now!" Al said huskily as he released her. He kissed her once more and said, "Go now, *Liebchen!*"

Emma turned around once. He looked back and called, "Don't worry!"

All she could hear as she walked was the cold snow squeaking under her feet. At first she thought about Al and how much she loved him, and then her thoughts swung back to her main concern. *What will I do if Jenny leaves? There could still be weeks of cold weather. Why doesn't Grandpa think of helping her? He knows she's in that cold schoolhouse every morning.*

But not once did she consider praying, not even when she went to bed that night.

Fourteen

The Promise of Spring

Monday morning Emma lovingly washed Jenny's white blouses and black poplin skirt. Earlier that morning she had asked Jenny if she could do any laundry for her.

"I didn't expect to have laundry service when I came here," Jenny had said. "But I'd certainly appreciate it. Evenings and Saturdays go so fast."

"It's a fair trade," Emma had replied. "You didn't expect to take care of the children as much as you do, either."

When she finished washing the blouses she wrung them in tight little rolls, washed the rest of the white clothes, and then rubbed Jenny's skirt on the washboard, carefully turning it this way and that. She wrung it, too, and laid it beside the blouses while she fixed the rinse water.

Then she put the blouses back into clean water to be rinsed. Oh, no! Emma couldn't believe her eyes! Where one blouse had touched the black skirt, there were ugly blue-black marks!

Quickly she put soap on the blouse and swished it in the water, aware that she would have to change the rinse water again. Hardly daring to breathe, she scrubbed the spots. They didn't budge. She scrubbed as hard as she dared without making a hole in the fabric, but it was no use! If it were summer, she could lay the blouse in the sun, but what could she do now?

Vinegar! I'll try vinegar. Carefully she laid the spotted section in a dish of vinegar and left it to soak a few minutes. The spots were as dark as ever. She couldn't think of anything else to try, so she rinsed it in fresh water and hung it up to dry.

Emma finished the laundry, feeling shaky and sick. How would she tell Jenny?

Well, she sighed. *There go our pleasant evenings. It could take her till spring to get over this. If only I had been more careful.* She could hear her father's gruff voice. "Saying 'I'm sorry' won't make the corn grow back," he had said the time she had carelessly left the gate open, and the cows had trampled and torn down rows and rows of corn.

If only Pa had said, "I forgive you. I know you're sorry," but he hadn't. For days he wouldn't even look at her, much less talk to her. Eventually he had forgotten about it and talked to her, and even joked with her again. But it had taken a long time.

She imagined Jenny tight-lipped and silent all through supper and the rest of the evening.

Anger, so overwhelming it frightened her, welled up inside, and she was glad she was going out to water the stock. "Why," she demanded of the gray sky, "are there such words as *I'm sorry* and *forgive me* if they don't work?"

One hopeful thought surfaced as she plodded back to the house. *Maybe the spots won't show when the blouse is dry. Spots always show more when cloth is wet.*

But the little flame of hope went out like a match by an open door when she got back in the house. The spots were as dark and ugly as ever, though the blouse was nearly dry.

Emma knew Jenny sensed that something was wrong before she had finished her syrup bread. *I might as well get it over with,* she told herself, as she took the blouse off the clothes rack behind the stove and brought it to Jenny.

"I know it doesn't help to say I'm sorry, but I am." Emma's voice broke.

"How did it happen?" Jenny asked quietly as she examined the spots.

When Emma explained, Jenny said, "It's funny I haven't done that myself. I've done so many other stupid things. Don't feel bad, Emma. I'll wear it around the house, if you don't mind looking at the stains."

Jenny hung the blouse back up to finish drying and began talking to the children as though nothing had happened.

Emma waited, tense-jawed. *Surely she'll suddenly realize that her good blouse is ruined, and then she'll be angry.* Emma had never known anyone not to be angry in a similar situation, not even Al. Although Al didn't stay sullen like her parents, it always took him a while to get over something she had done wrong.

But instead of ignoring Emma, Jenny put her arm around her shoulders and said, "Come! Sit down a minute. I have something to tell you."

Jenny's sparkling eyes banished all Emma's dread.

When they were settled at the table, Jenny said, "I could hardly wait to tell you. This morning I saw smoke coming out of the chimney before I got to school. I almost ran the rest of the way. Can you believe it—there was Grandpa Verleger stuffing wood in the stove! I could have hugged him!"

Emma's jaw dropped. "What did he say? Why did he—?"

"He said he couldn't stand to think of me in that cold schoolhouse one more morning. And, wait till you hear this! When he discovered there was hardly any kindling left, he went home and got a big arm load of his own and brought it over. He said he'll bring all I need this year."

Emma's mouth hung open, but Jenny chattered on. "He insisted that I come home with him until the room warmed up. Oh, Emma! Grandma Verleger tried so hard to be pleasant. She poured me a cup of real coffee—she always made barley coffee when I boarded there—and served it in a pretty china cup with roses on it. They didn't say so, but it was plain to see they missed me."

Emma shook her head in amazement.

"And that's not all! Grandpa insisted that he'll start the fire every morning, so I don't have to come so early, and I'm to come to their house whenever I want to until the schoolhouse gets warm."

She grabbed both Emma's hands. "Emma! Do you see? God has answered my prayers! *He* changed Grandpa's heart." She released Emma's hands and sat back with a sigh. "I knew He would."

Emma couldn't find words. She simply nodded and blinked back tears. She went about the evening's work in a blissful daze. *Jenny would be staying! There was no need to worry. God does answer prayers. Grandpa actually changed his mind.*

When the children were in bed, and the two women had settled down to read, Emma said, "I just can't believe you aren't mad at me about your blouse."

"Oh, Emma! I know you didn't do it purposely. And even if you had, I'd still forgive you."

Emma's eyes widened. "You would? How could you?"

"Christians don't have a choice. We must forgive."

"Must?

"Of course. In the Lord's Prayer, don't we ask God to forgive us the way we forgive others? Doesn't that mean that if we don't forgive others, we can't expect God to forgive us?"

"Oh, my goodness!" Emma's knitting lay idle. "I never thought of that."

"After all, God forgives us when we tell Him we're sorry and turn away from what we've done wrong, and purpose not to do it again." Jenny paged through her Bible and read, "If we confess our sins, he is faithful and just to forgive us our sins, and to cleanse us from all unrighteousness."

"Where does it say that?"

Jenny held the Bible so Emma could see for herself. "Right here in the ninth verse of the first chapter of the first letter of John."

Emma's thoughts whirled. Did that mean God forgave right away? Could she risk telling Jenny how she had been angry with God? She couldn't imagine Jenny's ever doubting God or refusing to pray, because He didn't do things the way she thought He should. How long would it take God to forget how she had acted toward Him? How would she know when it was all right to come to Him again?

Jenny was talking, but Emma was busy thinking. Then she heard Jenny say, ". . . and when He died for our sins and rose again, *all* our sins were paid for, so now when the Father looks at us—those of us who have accepted Jesus as our Savior and made Him Lord of our lives—He sees us covered with Jesus' righteousness. It's like we're wearing a robe of righteousness that covers all the sins we'll ever commit."

They talked a while longer. Eventually Jenny must have been confident that Emma understood what she had said. She read where she had left off in the Bible the night before, and then went on to read in *Little Women*, but Emma's thoughts were like leaves in the wind.

It was only after she was in bed that those thoughts began to settle down enough for her to put them in order.

After Jenny left Tuesday morning, Emma began thought-sorting again. She tried to remember the verse Jenny had read, but she was missing some of the words. She took the Bible over to the window and hunted for the first letter of John. Yes! There it was, "If we confess our sins, he is faithful and just to forgive us our sins, and to cleanse us from all unrighteousness."

Like a huge bubble, joy grew within her until she wanted to shout, "I'm forgiven! I was wrong—God isn't like Ma or Pa or Al. God is like Jenny—or rather, Jenny is like God, when it comes to forgiving. She forgives right away! And when God looks at me, He doesn't see me and all I've done wrong. He sees me through Jesus—and He's perfect!" She let out a gale of laughter that startled Albert.

He tugged at her apron. "What you laughin' at, Mama?"

She picked him up and whirled him around. "I just learned something *wonderful!* I'll teach you all about it, but it will take a while. I'll have to do it a little at a time."

She couldn't wait for Jenny to get home. She couldn't wait for Al to get home. There were still many pieces to fit in, she knew, but at least she was heading in the right direction.

At noon, when the little ones were asleep and Albert was contentedly playing, Emma slipped out to water the stock.

Nature wasn't presenting anything spectacular today. No sparkling fluffy new snow. No "floured" trees. Yet each curve of snow drift was a work of art, and the patch of blue sky beautiful beyond words. "The cover's off!" she shouted into the quiet air. "I don't just see it—I feel it!"

She let the cattle out and followed them down to the river, her heart singing. Soon it would be spring, and the violets would bloom along the river and the forget-me-nots would sprinkle blue all along the south side of the house. The boys would whoop and holler like little savages, and Ellie would patter along the hard dirt path with pudgy bare feet, giggling instead of whining. No more crying at the window. On warm days Emma would take them down to the sand bar in the river and let them splash and kick in the water to their hearts' content. She'd even stick little Georgie's feet in the water and watch him curl his little toes.

And Al would pull out more stumps, maybe with a team instead of the old ox, and soon there would be smooth fields, not just crops planted between the tree stumps. Sometimes Al would put his arm around her shoulders and point out, again, where he planned to build the new house. And he wouldn't have to go to camp all summer. In the evening, they'd sit under the stars listening to the crickets and the murmur of the river, and she'd feel there was nothing she couldn't face as long as they were together.

The cows were at the river waiting for their water. She hurried down the path and ducked under the fence and hoisted up an icy bucket of water. As she shoved it toward the ox, the realization flooded her: *I can pray again! I can talk to God. He isn't mad at me like I thought He was! He isn't frowning at me.* She began laughing and then laughed even more at the startled cows.

Where would she start? So much to thank Him for, so much to tell Him. . . .

Back up the hill she plodded behind the pokey old ox. She shut the stock in the barn and stood with her back against the barn door. The sun was warm on her face.

Emma closed her eyes. *Oh Father*, she whispered, *I missed You!*

If you enjoyed this book,
you'll want to read others stories in

The Never Miss a Sunset
Pioneer Family Series

Never Miss a Sunset
The second in the Pioneer Family series, set in the
very early 1900's, this wonderful classic is told
through the eyes of the oldest Verleger daughter,
Ellen. Here is a story for the entire family; it will
help build faith.

ISBN 1-55513-473-4   44735

All Things Heal in Time
In another story about this northern Wisconsin
family, Emma faces great adjustments when a
daughter dies and she is faced with the challenges
of raising the infant grandaughter. A wonderful
lesson in perseverence and overcoming.

ISBN 1-55513-484-X   44743

Available at your local Christian Bookstore

David C. Cook Publishing Company
850 North Grove
Elgin, Illinois 60120